BLOOD MOON BOUND

BLOOD MOON BRIDES, BOOK ONE

SHERILEE GRAY

Blood Moon Bound - Sherilee Gray - 2nd ed.

Epub ISBN: 978-1-99-118066-7

Print ISBN: 978-1-7386194-3-6

Special Edition Print ISBN: 978-1-99-118068-1

Prologue

CONSTANTINE

Five years ago

I GROUND MY MOLARS, every one of my muscles straining as pleasure-pain spiked down my spine and fizzed in my blood. I didn't know where I was going, only that I needed to get there, fast.

Pulling over on the side of the road, I got out of the car and let the sensation guide me. This was a vampire neighborhood and the street was lined with massive houses either side, people I had no interest in getting to know or spending time with, and right then, it was the only place I wanted to be.

I shook my head like an angry beast, trying to stop the constant pounding in my skull, like a metronome underwater. I shouldn't be out in public like this, not yet. I'd only just gotten back from months patrolling the fae border, and my body and mind were still there, on high alert, still amped to fight, to kill, to bleed my enemies. I was as far from civilized as I'd ever been.

There was no getting back in my car and going home, though, not with this deafening roar inside me, and the invisible fist that gripped my sternum, pulling me forward like I was a puppet on a string. It wouldn't relinquish its hold, and I was helpless to do anything but let it lead me where it will. I was tracking, hunting, but not the enemy, not this time.

The boulder in my gut told me exactly what this was, even if my mind refused to believe what my body was screaming. With every step, I scrambled to explain away everything I was feeling, but there was only one explanation.

My mate—she was calling me.

She was calling me to her and I doubted she even knew she was doing it.

The sound of a female humming reached me, stopping me dead in my tracks beside a thick hedge. Here. She was on the other side of this hedge. So close. I barely resisted tearing a hole in it and storming through, instead I forced myself to follow the tall hedge until I found a way in. There was a small gate a couple of yards ahead, one that obviously wasn't in use anymore, padlocked and overgrown. I snapped the rusted padlock, tossed it aside, then as quietly as I could, worked the gate free from the hedge trying to swallow it and walked through.

The humming was farther away now, but she was still close.

I moved quickly and silently through the garden, letting the grip around my dead, cold, unbeating heart lead me on. Moving in behind a small cluster of trees, I breathed deep, taking in her scent, letting it fill my lungs. She smelled like the roses she stood among, her own perfume even sweeter, more intoxicating. The constant pounding in my head—it was her, the slow steady beat of her heart, the rush of her blood. My mouth watered.

She stepped out from behind an ivy-covered gazebo and I got my first glimpse of her. Her head was tilted back, her black hair, a glossy, silky curtain despite the lack of sunshine. She was young, sixteen. I knew because that's how this worked, that was the earliest a male could detect his female. Not an average male, for them, this feeling tearing through me, came much later, but my brothers and I were not average males, we were old, and powerful —we were the exception—and my little mate would have no idea I existed.

She wouldn't even be able to hear me, even with her advanced hearing. My heart didn't beat, I had no need to breathe. Still, when she tilted her head back and smiled, I sucked breath into my lungs for no good reason and wished she'd turn her head and look at me. Christ, the delicate female in front of me had my body and mind going haywire.

My mate was...beautiful.

She held the rose in her small hand to her nose, breathing deep, a look on her face that caused the grip in my chest to tighten until it was almost unbearable. She continued to hum as she trailed her fingers over the roses in bloom all around her.

Every muscle in my body tightened as I fought to stay where I was and not snatch her up and take her away. She was too young, I knew it, but the urge to protect what was mine, was pounding through me so strongly, it was all I could feel.

As much as I wanted to stay right here, I needed to leave now and not come back. Staying close to her before it was time to claim her would only increase the bond between us, and she wasn't ready for that. Not mentally, and definitely not physically. But worse, as strong a male as I was, being this close to her and not mating her, could cause her pain, could ignite a need in her that she wasn't ready for and only I could ease. I could not, would not do that to her, not while she was so young and innocent.

My only choice was to leave, to walk away, and not come back until she was ready.

I'd dreamed of this day for so long, nights that were filled with screams and blood, she was the only thing that gave me peace, closing my eyes and imagining a sweet, little female all my own.

She was finally within my grasp, and come her twenty-first birthday she would be mine.

I was going to claim her, mate her, keep her, and I would never let her go.

One

DELPHINE

Five years later

AGATHA HELD up a towel as I climbed out of the tub. I wrapped it around myself, shivering, but not from the cold.

The night had finally arrived.

And nothing would ever be the same again.

I walked into the main room. My bedroom at home was opulent but nothing compared to the one here at the Grande Rozala. The hotel was beautiful, an ancient castle on the outskirts of Roxburgh, reserved for special occasions and ceremonies, and far enough from the city to feel like another place and time entirely.

"I'll get your dress, Miss Delphine. I've laid your underwear out on the bed."

I'd known Agatha all my life, she was the closest being I had to a friend, but she'd only ever treated me with cool detachment, as was expected. Friends were forbidden for someone such as me.

Tonight, all over Roxburgh, blood moon ceremonies were

taking place. Bondeds were being claimed by their mates, and their new lives were about to start. Their males would have sensed them, found them, then taken time to get to know them. They would have fallen in love, like most beings did.

My situation, though, was very different.

For some, like myself and the other four females here tonight, we'd never met the males coming for us, there'd been no getting to know each other, and our lives had not been our own.

The fates selected our mates when we turned sixteen. Only those of our kind who were old and extremely powerful had the ability to sense us that early. And if they did, and they so chose, they could announce their intent to claim their female when they came of age.

That happened to me, only instead of the male coming to our home and introducing himself, a member of the Vampire Court arrived the day after my sixteenth birthday and announced I'd been sensed by a male of great importance. No name was given, only that he was one of The Five.

I was kept safe after that. My stepfather and mother locked me away, making sure I remained unspoiled in every manner for the male who would come for me after I turned twenty-one. My life had already been controlled, restricted. My stepfather had hoped, no, planned for me to mate well, and he didn't want me "tainted" by the outside world. But his early efforts had been nothing compared to the restrictions of the last five years.

The identity of my mate remained a secret, even from my parents. We were told it was because of who he was—and for our safety, that's what my stepfather, Douglas, said, anyway—and after years of loneliness, the time had finally arrived to discover who he was.

Tonight, The Five were coming to claim their brides under the blood moon, and I was one of them.

The crunch of tires on gravel came from outside. I rushed to the window and watched as cars rolled in. Vampires from all over the city were here to celebrate the special occasion. The Five were warriors, the most ruthless, terrifying, and brutal vampires of our race, males who had patrolled the borders of our territory for hundreds of years, protecting our kind and laying waste to any who would dare try to harm us. They were spoken about among our people like a myth or legend, stories told to children at bedtime to make them feel safe.

To do their job, they needed the ability to travel in and out of our enemies' territories undetected, which was why their identities were such a closely guarded secret.

People speculated about who they were, of course, but no one ever knew for certain. What I did know was they were powerful males who moved in and out of society, never revealing who they really were, and therefore never getting the recognition they deserved for all they'd done for us.

All that changed tonight.

A new fae king had been crowned, and the war with the fae had ended. After fighting on and off for centuries, The Five were rejoining society for good.

I shuddered, but I wasn't sure if it was from fear or excitement.

I'd read several articles about them, things that had sent a shiver down my spine and fascinated me at the same time. I'd wanted to read more, but I'd never had control over what I watched or read, or who I spent time with. My stepfather had been trying to frighten me by sharing these articles, but it'd just made me more intrigued about my future mate.

Four town cars rolled in, pulling up outside the imposing castle. My heart raced.

Chauffeurs got out and rushed to open the doors. One by one, four massive vampires stepped out of their cars.

I sucked in a breath at the sight of them—power, dominance, menace saturated the air, even from this distance. They strode into the building, and the cars pulled away.

By the end of the night, I might be bride to one of them.

Music drifted up from below, voices, laughter.

The grandfather clock tolled, and I jumped.

Douglas would be here to collect me soon. With shaking hands, I dropped my towel and pulled on my underwear and the strapless corset laid out for me. I'd just secured my stockings when Agatha walked back in carrying my dress.

"Quickly now," she said, helping me lace up the corset before slipping the dress over my head. "Your stepfather will be here any minute."

The gown was red, the skirt heavy with layers of silk and tulle that flowed to the floor. The bodice was tightly fitted and all lace, and had a deep V that revealed the modest swell of my breasts.

What if the male I was destined for didn't like it or, worse, what if he saw me and didn't want me? The thought sent a shiver through my body. Yes, I was his mate, but mates were sometimes rejected. Douglas wouldn't countenance that kind of humiliation. He'd make me pay in ways I couldn't bear to think about.

"Did you see them?" I asked, not expecting Agatha to answer. She never went against my parents. She'd followed the rules of my upbringing to the letter. Her life would have been forfeit if she hadn't, and we both knew it.

But when she gently turned me, gone was my rigid and cool nanny, and in her place was the female I remembered from when I was very small. The female who had told me stories at bedtime and held me when I cried for my mother. The female who had squeezed my hand when I watched children playing, wanting to join them so desperately but hadn't been allowed.

Her lips curled up tentatively, shakily, and she smoothed a lock of my hair, then nodded. "I know you're afraid, Delphine, but you're strong and resilient, self-reliant. Embrace what is to come, make the most of the hand dealt to you." Her gaze softened. "Please, don't fight it. Your mate can make your life unpleasant if he chooses to. You don't want that."

Fear fired through me as she led me to the dressing table by the window and sat me down. I refused to give in to the fear. Whatever came next couldn't be worse than what I'd already endured. Years of loneliness and neglect, of mental abuse and manipulation. No, anything would be better than remaining here.

Agatha arranged my hair, leaving it loose in long, silky waves. She'd just finished applying my deep red lipstick when the sound of another car arriving reached us.

I shot out of my seat and ran to the window. "The last of The Five."

Agatha moved in beside me.

The door opened at the back of the car before the driver could get to it.

I froze, unable to look away.

The male who stepped out was huge. He had to be close to seven feet tall. His dark hair was slicked back, and when he straightened his tie with scarred, tattooed hands and did up his dinner jacket, the fabric over his broad shoulders and thick biceps strained.

He glanced up.

My breath caught as his eyes, the deepest violet, so dark they looked black, came right to me and held. I grabbed the window frame when my knees threatened to give out from under me.

A jagged scar ran down the side of his face, curving around his square jaw. The utterly terrifying male didn't blink, didn't smile, just stared right at me.

Then his lips peeled back, flashing sharp fangs. Not a smile, a sneer.

I darted back out of view, my hand flying to my chest. My gaze slid to the door as I envisioned myself shoving it open and running out of here, just running and never returning.

But that wasn't an option.

My stepfather would hunt me down and bring me back in a matter of hours. I'd humiliate and dishonor him, and he'd make me pay for it. I'd been told often that I was lucky, that I was special, that this was the kind of honor young females dreamed of.

Suddenly, I felt like a lamb going to slaughter, born only to feed a monster, to obey his demands without question or resistance.

There was an assertive knock at the door.

I grabbed the edge of the table as nerves exploded through me. I spun to Agatha, and her eyes were round and filled with concern.

"What is it?" My gaze sliced to the window, then back to her. "Do you know who that was?"

Lips trembling, she gave my shoulder a squeeze but didn't reply, then bustled to the door. She opened it, and Douglas stood there, tall and cold, immaculate in his dark tux.

I gathered my composure and turned fully toward him. Cold and cruel, he spent little time with me, except when he wanted to remind me of what was at stake, what would happen to me if I failed to fulfill my duty. I fought back a shudder of revulsion. He'd been so excited when we learned I was to mate one of The Five. My alliance tonight with one of those rich and powerful males would elevate his status, would gain him the respect he'd been hungry for all his life, and would make him rich when my mate gifted him a dowry in exchange for me, and that was all that mattered to him.

His gaze swept over me, and he gave me a short nod of approval before offering me his arm. "They're waiting."

Curling my fingers around his forearm, I let him lead me along the hall and down a sweeping staircase. The sound of voices, all talking over one another was louder now.

"My uncle is in attendance this evening. If you embarrass me in front of him, Delphine, in front of all these people, I will make you wish you were never born. Understand?"

His uncle sat on the Vampire Court and was a very important male. Douglas was always trying to impress him. He stopped suddenly, and grabbed my jaw, forcing me to look at him, and what I saw in his eyes made me quake with fear.

"The things you've seen in my dungeon will be nothing to what you would suffer," he snarled in my face, his eyes glowing, the thought of hurting me exciting him.

I nodded woodenly. I didn't need his warning, though. I would be leaving tonight, no matter what. I was nervous and scared, but out of all the monsters here tonight, my stepfather was worst of all.

Two

DELPHINE

MY MOTHER WAITED at the bottom of the stairs. When I reached her, she took my hand, pulling me aside before we could walk through the massive double doors that would lead into the ballroom. I didn't know why she stayed with Douglas; probably because, like a lot of our race, she was cold and calculating. Many vampires, especially the older ones, didn't possess the ability to feel emotion, and I wondered if my mother was older than she said. Mating, the process of falling in love, if love came when a couple mated, could bring those emotions back in older vampires, and maintain the ability if younger. That obviously never happened for the cold female staring down at me.

"Mother?" I used to crave affection from her—a hug, a simple touch—but it never happened. I couldn't remember her ever holding me.

"Your mate will demand certain things of you, Delphine. You must submit, always. Do as he says, follow his lead. Don't ask for things or be demanding. He will decide what's best for you. The five warriors here tonight hold positions of great power, are incredibly wealthy, and others will be jealous of you, of us, and the position you will hold by the end of the night. You must maintain that position at all cost, and that means keeping your male happy and satisfied in every way."

This was the first time I'd seen anything close to emotion from her. Concern. But not for me, for herself, and the possibility of losing what this alliance would give her if I failed somehow.

Four other young women and their fathers made their way down the hall. I'd wondered who the others would be, and there was no missing that they were all as terrified as me, but there was also the same glimmer of hope in the eyes of a few of them that I'd seen in my own. They were finally escaping the loneliness.

We were led to the doors and lined up, and I forced myself to hold my ground when one of the other females took a terrified step back, then quickly composed herself.

My mother's gaze swept over us all, and my stepfather took in the lineup, his spine straight, his gaze warning me not to embarrass him.

Two young males stepped forward and pushed the double doors wide.

The talking in the room stopped, and every set of eyes locked on us.

One of the males stepped forward and began to announce us, introducing us to the gathered crowd, telling them who our families were since no one had laid eyes on us for the last five years, hidden away as we'd been.

I suddenly felt faint. *You can do this. You have to do this.*

"Miss Delphine Albertan. Daughter of Douglas and Miriam Albertan." On shaky legs, I stepped forward.

The air seemed to vibrate, humming with energy as if electricity were dancing across my skin. From the corner of my eye, I saw my parents step forward, inclining their heads to the crowd. But I didn't turn to look. I kept my gaze trained straight ahead like I'd been told to do.

"Now, please welcome our honored guests. Warriors all, and

protectors of our race," the male by the door announced. "Stefan Valiente, Rainer Beiste, August Drapała, Nero Kossek—"

The crowd of vampires stepped back quickly as, one by one, the warriors strode into the room. My heart pounded, and the way their gazes raked over us as they entered the room—hungry, predatory—I knew I couldn't be the only one silently terrified. Where was the fifth?

The vampires standing opposite us were the only ones who knew which of us would be their bride. My gaze flew over them. Which one? Which one would be my mate? Confusion rumbled through the room, because a male was missing, and there was now one female too many.

One of the warriors broke away from the group. My heart hammered as he walked toward me, but then he stopped in front of the female on my right, greeted her, and led her away from the lineup.

The next came forward, and then the next—

Until I was the only one standing there.

The room went utterly silent. Had my mate decided he didn't want me? Everyone else had to think it. Humiliation burned my face. My gaze went to Douglas, and the fury in his eyes almost had my legs collapsing beneath me. Oh god, somehow, he would make this my fault and I would pay for it. He'd make good on his promise. It was over for me. He wouldn't need to keep me scar-free anymore, and the twisted look in his eyes told me he knew it as well.

No.

Run, my mind screamed. *Run as fast as you can.*

I took a step back—

The sound of boots on the glossy marble floor echoed through the silent room.

"The final member of The Five, their esteemed commander, Constantine Caputo."

A gasp was the only sound that followed that pronouncement.

My mother's. I froze, not looking up, because I knew what I'd see. Who I'd see. The footsteps drew nearer, and my heart pounded so hard I felt faint.

Extremely large boots filled my vision, but still I didn't look up.

Oh god.

Seconds ticked by.

"Look at me," an impossibly rough voice finally said.

I had no choice. I lifted my chin, tilting my head back, and looked up into the scarred face of the massive vampire I'd seen through the window.

His cold eyes locked on mine. "Delphine," the dark-eyed vampire said and took my hand, bringing it to his perfectly sculpted lips. A shot of electricity bolted through me at the contact.

This male, this monster, had no idea that he was my savior. I only hoped he didn't want to be my jailor as well.

Music began, and we were led to the dance floor inside a huge glass-walled sunroom off the main room. There would be just one, my first real dance, before we'd be taken away and whatever was supposed to happen to bind us under the blood moon would happen.

He pulled me against him, and I was close to hyperventilating. He was so incredibly tall, and there was no missing the immense power in his body as he held me to him, muscles straining against his jacket and trousers. Under the civilized suit was no gentleman. No, my mate was a commander, a brutal warrior, and a vicious and relentless killer.

And now I belonged to him.

He could do whatever he wanted to me, and I would have no choice but to let him.

He dipped his head. "You tremble like a frightened rabbit. Are you nervous, Delphine?"

I jumped, unable to stop myself. "Yes." There was no point

lying. There was no hiding it, not from this male. He would hear it, smell it, sense it.

He glided me easily around the dance floor despite his size. "You know what's to come?"

His voice had grown deeper, rougher, and I picked up an accent.

I shook my head.

He growled, and his mouth dipped to my ear. "I'll make sure you like it, bride." My breath caught, and he chuckled darkly.

I forced myself to look up at him and knew I was wide-eyed and breathless, but there was nothing to be done about it. "You're to be my mate, what should I call you?"

He smiled. It wasn't pleasant. "Constantine."

I realized I'd seen this male before. Just once. Douglas had left his laptop open on the table after breakfast one morning. When I'd walked by, a picture had caught my eye.

I'd frozen in place, taking in the bloody, battle-scarred vampire standing there. I'd studied every visible inch of him. The commander of The Five. His face had been concealed, of course, but I knew now that it was Constantine. He'd ventured into the fae realm after their king had threatened to murder several of our elders, making it clear they wouldn't stop there, that they'd keep going until the river that ran between them and us had turned red with vampire blood. Constantine had spent months in enemy territory.

He'd returned with their king's head.

I hadn't recognized him in his suit, his face clean-shaven. But my mate-to-be was the most vicious male our race had ever seen.

My gaze flew to my stepfather. He stood there watching us, fury burning in his eyes. This was what he'd wanted.

Then why did he look so angry?

The song ended, and I stood frozen as the sunroom roof slid back, revealing the blood moon, its red glow shining down on us. When I looked back up at Constantine, all traces of civility had washed from his face. I was looking at a monster, a monster who was about to take a bite out of me.

One by one, the girls were lifted off the ground, their cries of fear and surprise spiking terror through me as they were carried from the ballroom.

"You'll have to excuse my brothers," Constantine said. "Some of us have been at war for so very long, without blood, without females, with only death and vengeance to keep us warm." He breathed deeply. "And you smell...so very good."

My gaze flew across the room, finding my parents again. Someone was handing Douglas a piece of paper. He looked down at it, and fury instantly filled his eyes.

"Time for the letting, little one," Constantine said.

"The letting?"

Douglas strode forward, his gaze darting to his uncle, then back to Constantine. He looked up at the huge warrior still holding me close, his anger obvious, though he was trying to hide it in front of our audience. "This won't stand."

Constantine grinned. "Is there a problem, Douglas?"

"You can't have her," my stepfather said.

"She's already mine."

"W-what's going on?" Unease filled me at the anger I felt radiating from both males, and I took a step back.

Constantine thwarted my retreat with one of those massive hands around my wrist and pulled me back in.

"Is there a problem here?" Douglas's uncle said, joining us.

My stepfather's expression changed instantly, the anger dropping from his face, and he smiled. "No, problem. Just offering my congratulations."

His uncle's brows lowered. "It's not done, Douglas. You're interrupting the ceremony."

My stepfather flushed. "Apologies. My emotions got the better of me."

His uncle ushered him back to my mother, and I couldn't stop myself from taking another retreating step. Again, Constantine halted me, then dipped his head. "No one here will save you, little rabbit. But if you run, I'd very much enjoy catching you."

He sounded so calm, even as the hunger in his eyes burned brighter. "Are you going to hurt me?" I asked.

"Only a little."

There was no concealing the fear now.

"Are you going to walk out of here with me, Delphine, or will I have to carry you?"

Fighting would only make this worse. So I straightened my spine. "I'll walk."

He gripped my elbow as if he expected me to make a run for it anyway, like one of the other girls had, but I knew how pointless that would be.

There was no outrunning this male.

Three

DELPHINE

Constantine's grip was firm as he strode through the maze of gardens behind the castle, leading me deeper and deeper into the grounds. A scream of terror made me jump. It came from one of the brides, and was not the first I'd heard since we left the castle. Oh god, what was happening to them? What was about to happen to me? But then the screams faded, and in their place, moans and growls filled the night.

Those sounds were not from pain but pleasure.

My heart hammered in my chest, and the cool night air lifted goose bumps across my flesh. Constantine strode on, his grip on my wrist unrelenting as I stumbled after him. Soon, I could no longer hear the others. We were all alone.

He stopped in a small clearing surrounded by dense trees that blocked the cool breeze and formed shadows that made the garden look as if it were draped in black lace.

The silence was heavy. The only sound now, my wild breaths. The perfume of lavender filled my head, mixed with something dark and rich—Constantine.

"Your heart is beating so fast, little one, what do you think I'm going to do to you?" he said, his voice a low rumble.

"I…I don't know."

"No one told you?"

I shook my head, the racing of my heart making me dizzy.

Long, cool fingers gripped my chin and angled it, tilting it to the side. He gripped my throat with the other hand lightly before slowly sliding it lower. His thumb brushed over the fluttering vein there. "I'm going to sink my fangs into your virgin skin and drink."

There was no stopping the way his words made me tremble. I was a confusion of thoughts and feelings. Fear was there, and something else, something that made my belly swirl and tiny electric zaps shoot through my veins. I'd heard the screams of the others, but I'd also heard their moans of pleasure. "Will it hurt?"

His violet eyes bore into me. "Only if I want it to."

I fought my fear. I could take it. Whatever came next, I could take it. I wouldn't let it break me. The alternative, remaining with my stepfather, was so much worse. I gathered my courage. "And do you…want to hurt me?"

His gaze traveled over my face, dipping to my mouth, then slowly lifted again, locking on to mine. He still had hold of my chin, and he lowered his face to mine. His scent filled my head, so rich and enticing.

He was utterly still, silent. I couldn't even hear the sound of his heart because it wasn't beating, which meant he was either extremely old or at some point had been so weak and starved, or so badly injured, that his heart had stopped. Somehow I knew, even though he was old, it was the latter.

He didn't answer. His cool cheek touched mine, and I jumped, then I felt his lips at my jaw, sliding lower. One of his fangs lightly scraped my skin, and I whimpered and grabbed his arm, terror filling me. His biceps bunched, then he sucked hard on my skin. I tried to pull away, but he held me fast.

"Don't move," he said harshly.

I swallowed, trembling as his lips moved lower, down to the

fluttering vein at the side of my throat. He stilled, then breathed deeply. A low sound, a growl rumbled through his chest.

"C-Constantine?"

He struck.

I screamed and dug my nails into his arms, not knowing if I wanted to shove him away or pull him closer as heat pooled at my throat, where he sucked greedily on my vein, stealing the breath from my lungs. The heat slid lower across my chest, blazing a path through my belly, then arrowing between my thighs. Heat pulsed... no, throbbed there, rippling inside me, causing muscles I never knew existed to clench, in the place I'd been forbidden to ever touch. My underwear grew damp. Oh god, I could feel a slickness on my inner thighs. What was happening to me? I slammed them together.

A strange and fierce hunger, foreign and all-consuming, had me pulling the brutal, utterly terrifying warrior closer to me, instead of shoving him away. The place between my thighs throbbed deeper, ached—god, it felt empty. I needed something I didn't understand. Right then, my body didn't belong to me. I was spinning out of control. Constantine still gripped my throat with one hand and my hip with the other, and he squeezed when I moaned, pressing myself against his hard body, reaching for something I couldn't name.

"That's it, little one, give in," he growled against my skin.

What did he want me to give in to?

The sensation low in my belly and between my thighs grew higher still. I cried out helplessly, trembling as I reached for it, whatever it was, and terrified of it at the same time. It grew so big, so vast I thought I was going to explode into a million pieces—

I shattered, screaming as pleasure like nothing I'd ever experienced crashed over me, wave after wave rocking through my body, causing muscles I never knew I had inside me to spasm repeatedly. My heart pounded, my skin was damp with perspiration, my thighs humiliatingly slick from whatever had just happened.

Embarrassment burned my cheeks even as that part of me continued to throb in a way I couldn't describe and didn't understand.

Constantine dragged his tongue over my throat and lifted his head. "You taste as delicious as I imagined." His nostrils flared as he scented me. "Did you make a mess, Delphine?"

My face burned hotter, and I couldn't meet his eyes. "I...I don't know what happened. I...I don't know..."

He pressed a thick finger to my lips, silencing me, and began gathering up the skirts of my dress. "Let me take a look and see what you've done to yourself."

"Please...don't."

He froze, his nostrils flaring before he dropped my dress.

There was a whistling sound. I spun—

Constantine threw me to the ground, his mouth pressing to my ear. "Don't move."

Then he was gone, so fast he was nothing but a blur. A scream rang out a moment later. It was unlike those I'd heard earlier. This was male, and it was a cry of pain...and terror.

Then Constantine was back. With a snarl, he lifted me, threw me over his wide shoulder, and ran. He growled something, and I realized he was talking to someone on his phone.

"What's going on?" I cried as he ran, so fast the world blurred past us.

"Your stepfather sent someone to kill me," he said.

Oh god.

Instead of going back to the castle, he ran through the land surrounding it, and when we reached the road, a car sped up to us. He bundled me into the back seat, climbed in beside me, and the car sped off.

He said nothing, still and silent beside me. I expected anger in his eyes, fury—what I saw instead was triumph.

My heart was pounding wildly. "Why would he do that?" I dared to ask.

Constantine turned to me. "Because he wants you back."

"But why?" My fear increased to a point I was close to hyperventilating.

"Because I made it clear he'll get nothing from me. None of the benefits he expected when he said yes to his daughter becoming a monster's bride." His gaze slid over me. "He wants his property back, possibly to find a more profitable prospect for you."

No wonder Douglas was furious. "Why won't you pay him a dowry?"

"That's not something you need to worry about, little rabbit."

Constantine had just made an enemy of Douglas, a male who, unlike my mother, wasn't completely emotionless; hate, jealousy, greed, cruelty, he felt all of them, acutely. The brooding warrior beside me was right. I was property, only ever something to be bartered. He wouldn't countenance this. "Can he...can he do that? Take me back?" Oh, god, please say no. I couldn't endure another moment in that house filled with fear and horror and loneliness. And after this, it would be so much worse. He'd take this out on me.

Constantine's deep violet eyes locked on mine. "Oh no, he won't be taking you back." He licked his lips. "I tasted you under the blood moon." He flashed his fangs. "There is no going back."

I nodded and quickly looked away, unable to hold that intense gaze as relief washed through me. I gripped the armrest and stared out the window, and my relief grew the farther we got from that castle and my parents.

I felt Constantine watching me, studying me. Did he expect me to scream and protest? Or beg him to take me back to my family? That would never happen. No matter what came next, nothing could drive me back to them.

Nothing.

～

I woke as Constantine laid me down. I blinked up at him. The room was dimly lit, his face mainly in shadow. "Where am I?"

"My home," he said and stepped back.

A low rumble rolled through the room, then crashed. I jumped. Thunder. I looked to the window. It was dark outside, the blood moon still high in the sky, but there were clouds gathering, a storm moving in fast.

I searched the room. The walls were stone and dark wooden panels. There was a wardrobe and dresser, also in dark wood, as was the bed I was on. I flexed my fingers against the velvet bedcover. It was the deepest of red, like the open curtains.

I didn't know what happened now, but whatever it was, no matter how nervous and afraid I was, I had to please him. I didn't want to give him any excuse to throw me out. It had to be safer here than out there on my own with no money or protection, or anyone I could trust.

Lightning forked through the sky, and the shadows and light created were a stark contrast, highlighting the sharp angles of Constantine's scarred face. His eyes glittered as he stared down at me.

When the silence became too much, I forced myself to speak. "I am at your service. Please tell me what you'd like me to do?" My voice shook embarrassingly, but there was nothing I could do about that.

I'd do anything to keep him from sending me home. He said there was no going back, but he could change his mind. If I didn't please him, he could toss me out.

"We need to complete the blood bonding before the moon sets," he said, and his voice was impossibly low and rough. His scarred hands went to the buttons of his shirt, and he began undoing them, exposing his deeply tanned throat and tattooed skin.

Heat burned my cheeks and I looked away.

"Have you never seen a male's chest?" The bed dipped when he sat on the edge.

I shook my head.

"Look at me."

My embarrassment grew, but I forced myself to do as he demanded. His shoulders were wide, his chest smooth and stomach roped with muscle and covered in tattoos. I had the strangest urge to reach out and touch, touch the expanse of smooth, decorated skin bared to me.

"How do you usually feed, little one?"

His voice rumbled, lifting goose bumps all over me. "A glass, and never from the same donor twice," I said quickly. When a vampire drank exclusively from one person, a bond could be formed. When a female turned sixteen, they developed their need to feed. Because I'd already been claimed, I was never permitted to feed directly from anyone. When I did, it would only be from my mate—from the brutal warrior staring down at me.

"You will drink from me now," he said.

My gaze sliced to his. Feed from him? Press my mouth against his skin, sink my fangs into his flesh, and drink directly from his vein? No. I couldn't, could I?

His throat was thick, the veins there also. My mouth watered, and hunger, sudden and urgent, yawned wide inside me. My stomach rumbled and heat hit my face. "A cup is fine," I said, an unmistakable tremble in my voice. "I wouldn't want to...you don't have to..." I swallowed hard. "I mean, unless you want..." I was rambling, trembling, at the thought of how close I'd have to get to Constantine to do what he asked of me.

"No cup." He crooked a finger. "Come here."

There was no escaping this. My face burned hotter. If we didn't complete the bonding ritual, I wouldn't be safe from my stepfather. Constantine was terrifying, but I didn't think he was vindictive or evil. I'd seen firsthand what that looked like.

Trembling, I climbed to my knees and shifted closer, then

stopped, not sure what to do. Constantine wrapped his large hands around my waist, and I gasped as he lifted me, planting me across his lap. I kept my head down, not knowing where to put my hands, where to look, what to do.

His skin was cool, I felt it through my clothes.

"Straddle me," he said.

He wanted me to...oh, god. I thought I might actually die of embarrassment. I didn't move.

"Now, Delphine."

It was an order, a demand. He was cold with me but not cruel. Would that change if I disobeyed him? Angered him? I didn't want to find out. Still trembling, I obeyed, shifting on his lap, forced to grip his shoulders as I repositioned myself. A whimper of humiliation slipped from me, though, as I spread my thighs around his.

I sat far enough back that I was almost perched on his knees, not wanting to get too close.

"Look at me," he said.

I couldn't, not while his eyes burned like flames, scorching across my flesh. Even with my dress covering the most intimate part of me, I felt vulnerable and exposed.

He growled, then those battle-scarred hands gripped my hips again, and he lifted me, putting me down so close to him our stomachs and chests collided. Another whimper escaped without my say so.

"Look at me," he said again.

I couldn't.

One of those thick, rough-skinned fingers slid under my chin, and he tilted my head back. "I don't have time to ease you into this, bride."

He grabbed something from his pocket, a knife, and flicked it open. I gasped and tried to jerk back, but he held me fast with one strong arm locked around me.

"Please...please, don't hurt me," the plea fell from my lips.

Constantine's gaze turned frigid. "I'm not your stepfather. I don't hurt females." Then, without flinching, he pressed the blade to the side of his throat. Blood immediately bubbled to the surface.

He tossed the knife to the bedside table. The scent hit me and I jolted as if struck, my fangs punching through my gums.

I breathed deep and my mouth watered.

"No blood you've ever had before will come close to mine," he said.

Something snapped inside me, all fear and embarrassment giving way to ravenous hunger, to tasting Constantine's blood. My hands flew to his shoulders and my nails dug into his flesh all on their own.

"Drink," he said roughly.

It was as if someone else had control over my body. I all but climbed him, licking up the trail of blood that had slid down the side of his neck, pooling at his collarbone, then covering the small slice in the side of his throat with my mouth. My vision turned red, my hunger becoming unbearable. Instinct took over and I struck, my fangs sinking deep into the thick, pulsing vein against my tongue. As soon as I withdrew them, his blood, rich and decadent, filled my mouth.

I swallowed and groaned wantonly, wriggling to get closer as I drew deep on his vein. My arms banded around his neck tighter, holding him there, afraid he'd pull away or try to stop me.

My breasts felt swollen, my nipples tight and sensitive. Heat pooled in my lower belly, and the secret place between my thighs began to pulse and grow damp again. There was something hard beneath me, and I pressed down on it, trying to ease the unbearable ache growing deep inside me.

Constantine gripped my hips more firmly, pushing me down against the hardness behind the zipper of his trousers with a growl. "That's it, little one."

At his roughly spoken words, I squirmed against him. The movement sent a wash of pleasure through me. It gathered between my legs and sent shockwaves through my belly. My nipples ached, and I hugged him tighter, pressing my breasts against the hard wall of his chest, desperate to ease the ache there as well.

I was lost in a red haze of hunger, of chasing the foreign sensations pulsing through my body. My hips rolled, and again, Constantine pressed me down against the hardness in his trousers.

My nails clawed and tore at his shoulders and back, my hips frantically moving against him as I smashed my breasts to his chest and sucked on his vein, drinking him down. That feeling built inside me again, making me tremble as ever heightening waves of pleasure built inside, just like they had in the garden when Constantine had fed from me, then it crashed—

I threw my head back and screamed, shaking and rocking against him like an animal without restraint or shame. I felt a gush of fluid between my trembling thighs, then another wave hit me, making me cry out a second time before I finally, helplessly, collapsed against the powerful male under me.

His breathing was harsh, his fingers still gripping my hip hard enough to leave bruises.

I lay against him, weak and drowsy, as I slowly became aware of the way I still touched him, of how close we were, his scent now branded on my senses—his decadent taste still on my tongue.

Oh god, the way I'd behaved. I tried to pull away.

Constantine held me fast. "Lick," he rumbled.

Blood lazily slid from the puncture wounds I'd made. I hadn't sealed them. I licked, another jolt sliding through me when his blood coated my tongue again. I wanted to pull away, but suddenly I was boneless, exhaustion hitting me hard and fast.

One of Constantine's hands slid up my thigh, swiping over my soaked underwear. I was too weak to even try to pull away. He growled something under his breath, then lifted me, jerked back the covers, and placed me roughly on the bed. I fought to keep my eyes open as he yanked them over me, then strode across the room to draw the curtains.

"Sleep," he said when he came back, then switched off the bedside lamp.

The sound of his retreating steps came next.

I opened my mouth to bid him good night, but the door closed behind him before I could.

Four

CONSTANTINE

I couldn't leave. I'd tried repeatedly to walk away from her door. I couldn't do it.

A growl tried to crawl up my throat and I forced it back down. Delphine was asleep and I didn't want to wake her. I didn't want her to open her door and find me still here. But mostly, I didn't want her opening the door because if she did, in my current state, I would grab her, toss her on the bed and finish what we'd started. I'd take her, mate her, bite her. I'd claim her in all the ways I'd dreamed about since I first laid eyes on her. Delphine was supposed to be my reward after centuries of war and bloodshed, but everything had changed and I couldn't have her, not like that, not the way I'd always imagined—not anymore.

We were blood bound, which for a female, stopped them suffering the way I currently was. If we remained unmated now, she'd be fine. It was the opposite for a male, it intensified the need to fuck, to *mate*, to complete the bond between us, which was why I was standing at her door, hard as steel, salivating from the scent of her pussy and her blood that was still all over me.

Resisting the driving need to mate my little bride was quickly becoming the hardest battle I'd ever faced. My skin was coated in a layer of sweat, my gut had a fucking rock in it, and my fangs wouldn't retract—and my cock was so painful I was struggling to fucking breathe, touching it pure agony, because what I was doing, resisting her this way, went against the laws of nature.

I just had to ride it out, resist her for a few days, when things would die down to a dull roar instead of this hellfire burning through me and eating me alive. Yes, I'd still want to fuck her all the time, but controlling it would be easier. I'd at least be able to function.

I unconsciously shifted my shoulders, expecting the pull against my skin from the marks she'd left, clawing at my back and shoulders, but they were gone, already healed. I had to bite back a growl. I wanted them back.

Light was beginning to fill my home. I'd been standing here the entire night.

Delphine made a sound, a little sigh, and I pressed my ear to the door, greedy to hear her voice. There was a rustle of covers and her scent grew heavier. She'd thrown them back. She'd gone to sleep in her dress, those soaking wet panties and I could smell her pussy more strongly now. My cock throbbed harder.

The sound of her small feet padding around the room, then drawing back the curtains came next.

Move. Walk away. Now.

My feet refused. This wasn't me. I was a master of self-control. Cold, deadly, unmatched on the battle field. I gritted my teeth. I would not be conquered by the tiny female on the other side of that door.

Her footsteps grew closer.

Move.

She was right fucking there, only a slab of wood between us.

Walk the fuck away.

The door opened.

Delphine gasped, her gaze slicing up to me, looking at me wide-eyed and terrified as I loomed over her like a fucking salivating monster. Her scent slammed into me, and the sound of her racing pulse, the pounding of her heart, filled my head. My mouth watered and I licked down one of my fangs. Why was I resisting her, again? I was struggling to remember. All I knew was that I needed to end this driving hunger.

"C-Constantine?"

Her voice slammed into my sternum with the force of a sledge-hammer, decimating the haze I was in. I gripped the doorframe to hold myself back. The wood creaked, on the verge of snapping in my hand. I needed to say something, find the words, any words, but none would come. I tried again, but all that came out was a snarl.

She skittered back, and I barely stopped myself from going after her, from pouncing on her.

It took every bit of strength I had, but I peeled my fingers from the doorframe and pushed myself back, then I forced myself to turn from her and walk away.

Before I did something I couldn't take back.

~

I could fucking smell her.

Delphine had been in my home for a week, and it was as if she'd quietly taken ownership of every square foot.

I paced my study.

I'd somewhat successfully avoided her since I brought her home. I'd had no choice, not after what happened the night she drank from me. I'd tried so fucking hard, but no matter what I did, I couldn't forget the way Delphine had clung to me, clawed at me, going wild from the taste of my blood.

That night, I'd wanted to tear off her soaked panties and drive deep inside her. I'd wanted to mate her and claim her in every way. That was not the plan, though. Not anymore.

I strode to the window and stared out at the first rays of

morning sun. I'd spent another night wearing out the fucking carpet in this room, because walking past her bedroom wasn't something I was sure I could do. I was afraid I'd walk in, climb under the covers with her, and *take her. Bite her.*

She was born to be mine, but I'd never imagined wanting her the way I did. What the fuck did I want with an innocent little female like that? I wanted Samara back. I wanted revenge against Douglas fucking Albertan, for what he did to her.

Samara had been the complete opposite of Delphine, experienced, sharp-tongued, ruthless. She hadn't trembled when I'd looked her in the eyes, or shied away in fear and disgust. She'd been perfect for me, the commander of The Five, a ruthless and ugly heartless monster—but fate had other plans for me. They chose someone else. And those evil bitches were probably laughing right now watching me fucking squirm and hide from the tiny, frightened female who had taken over my fucking house without even trying.

Samara and I had met when we were young, both homeless, living on the streets. I became her friend and protector. Over the years our relationship changed. When we found ourselves together, we shared each other's beds. I'd never demanded or even wanted faithfulness from her, and neither had she from me, because that's not what we had. Or at least, I believed that's the way she felt about me.

But Samara had been there for me, had gotten me through some of the hardest times of my life. She'd tended my wounds, slaked my lust, and fed me from her vein when I'd return from war broken and half wild. She held me and listened to the stories, nightmares really, from my time away that I couldn't flush from my mind until I spoke them aloud.

I couldn't let Delphine distract me from my goal. Samara was dead, and though I couldn't prove it, I knew Douglas was behind it. My position, my service to our people didn't change that killing another vampire without hard evidence, especially one with an uncle sitting on the Vampire Court, would be signing my own death warrant—and those of my brothers, because they wouldn't stand by and watch me be executed. It was for them that I hadn't already torn that fucker to pieces. It was for them that I'd bided my time, waiting for my chance to strike.

A memory rushed back, unbidden, of a time when I thought my life could be different.

The night I'd felt Delphine for the first time.

The monster had been driven by instinct, by something I'd never felt before—by the call of its mate. I'd tried to tell myself I just wanted one look at her, then I'd leave, that I wouldn't declare my intention to claim her—but then I'd seen her, so young, so fragile, so sweet and lovely. So breakable.

Still struggling to find my humanity again after months fighting, the monster had been firmly in charge, which was why I'd let instinct take hold and snuck into the Albertans' garden. The rapturous look in her eyes while she'd stood among her roses, breathing in their scent, had set off a possessive roar inside me that had been too much to resist. I'd almost snatched her from her stepfather's garden then.

I'd seen what could happen to young females like her when the enemy got hold of them, and that's all I could see—Delphine bloody and broken. I'd needed her safe.

And there was only one way to make sure of it.

Declare my intention to claim her. I'd been desperate to keep her safe, and knew her family would lock her down, so no harm could come to her, when I did. Then, still under her spell and utterly fucking besotted, I'd ordered rose gardens to be planted all over the grounds of my home.

For some reason, I'd kept it from Samara. I'd finally told her eighteen months ago. She said she was happy for me, but I could tell it bothered her. Not because she wanted me for herself but because she was afraid I'd abandon her like everyone else in her life had. I tried to reassure her that I'd always be there for her, but something changed between us, and I didn't know how to make it right.

We'd gone to a club that night, the kind that Samara enjoyed, the kind that smelled of sex and was filled with screams of both pleasure and pain. Samara introduced me to a male named Pere. Douglas had been in his entourage, along with several others who'd looked at Samara like she was prey. I hadn't liked it—and at the time, had no idea Douglas was Delphine's stepfather.

I'd stayed to make sure Samara was safe, even though I knew she'd been there many times without me and that she could take care of herself. I'd seen the way Douglas had watched her, a look on his face that had unsettled me as Pere had tied Samara up, choked her, whipped her, fucked her. She'd loved it, begging me to join in. I'd turned her down, then I'd carried her home afterward, and she'd drowsily begged me not to leave her before she'd fallen asleep.

That was the last time I'd seen her.

I'd been sent back to the border early that morning, and I hadn't had a chance to say goodbye. A month later I received word of her death. I found out Samara had been spending a lot more time with Pere and his friends, and that one of them had a private dungeon.

But Samara wasn't the only female to go missing after spending time with these males. And I'd fucking driven her to it. I'd hurt her, had been careless with her feelings, and she'd worked through them the only way she knew how, at that club, in that dungeon. I'd spoken to some of the regulars there and discovered it was Douglas's house, and the night of her death, she'd turned him down flat, humiliating him in front of his friends.

That was the last time anyone saw her.

I'd confronted Douglas, threatened him, but I wasn't at war anymore. I couldn't just kill my enemy and walk away, and with his uncle on the court, he was untouchable without any real proof of his guilt.

It wasn't until I'd found out where he lived that I realized it was the same house I'd seen Delphine.

I strode from the window and back. Yes, I'd obviously fucked off the fates somewhere along the way, because I couldn't see why else they'd do this to me?

Everything had changed after that.

My thirst for revenge had overridden everything else. Proving what Douglas did, making him pay became everything.

And Delphine became my means to an end.

She'd become my way of tipping Douglas over the edge, of sending him into a rage, of making a mistake and publicly giving me the reason I needed to execute him.

Walking into that castle and taking Delphine—his stepdaughter, his most prized possession—from him, and right under his fucking nose, had felt as good as I'd hoped. The piece of shit had reacted as I'd predicted the moment he realized who had come for her. That the money and the accolades, the connections and rise in society he thought was coming to him when Delphine mated one of The Five, wouldn't be coming.

Now he wanted me dead, so badly he'd sent an assassin after me the night of the ceremony, while I'd been fucking blood drunk on the taste of his sweet little stepdaughter. I should have been prepared for it. I still couldn't believe I'd momentarily dropped my guard.

I couldn't let it happen again. It was only a matter of time before Albertan sent someone else after me, giving me a reason, in the eyes of the Vampire Court, to finally execute him.

I'd thought about all these things, planned for them. What I hadn't thought about or planned for, was what would happen once I had Delphine here with me. I had no defense, no battle plan to fight the way I felt around her. Christ, feelings I hadn't experienced in too long to remember were slowly but surely reawakening. The way I'd lost my damn mind when she'd straddled me and sunk her delicate little fangs into my vein, drinking from me for the first time. The way she got lost in the taste of my blood, of chasing the first flames of her desire.

Christ, that hadn't been a mere awakening. Delphine had detonated in my arms. Pussy so drenched she'd soaked my pants, coming hard twice for me.

I shoved my fingers through my hair. I couldn't allow myself to have this female. She'd never be my mate in truth, I wouldn't allow it. The moment I had what I needed to destroy Douglas, I would leave. Leave her to get on with her own life.

The war may be over, but I was still a warrior. Taking a mate, that kind of life, it wasn't for me. I'd given up that dream when Samara was murdered and I learned who was behind it.

I wouldn't despoil her memory, not with the stepdaughter of the sadistic male who'd ended her life.

I'd never forgive myself for it.

It was early evening when I finally left my office. I needed a shower and some fucking sleep, but the clink of cutlery had me pausing outside the dining room, and though I knew who I'd see, I couldn't resist stopping in the doorway for a greedy glimpse of her.

Delphine, wearing a bright dress, her dark hair shining, a long silken curtain hanging down her back, sat at my enormous mahogany table. Under the muted light, she looked like a bright and shining star in a dark and moody night sky.

Platters of food were spread out in front of her, more than she could eat on her own. Her plate had only a few things on it. I enjoyed a meal a few times a week, not because I required it but because I liked the taste. Delphine was still young enough that she needed to have human food more often, though.

As for blood, I craved it less than her thanks to several lifetimes of war and being forced to go without. I also had the kind of self-control that only came with age. When I needed to feed now, I went to The Vault, my brother Nero's feeding club in the city, where people who wanted to be bitten offered themselves to blood drinkers. My gaze slid to Delphine's slender throat, and my mouth went dry. The idea of feeding from anyone else, alarmingly, no longer appealed.

No, the little female, the memory of her taste, was fucking with that self-control and driving me near feral with hunger.

She glanced up then, spotting me watching her. Color hit her cheeks instantly, and she quickly looked down. *Walk away.* That's what I should do, but my feet carried me into the room all on their own. Her innocence called to the predator in me, and the urge to play with my prey before I pounced, pounded through me.

And her refusal to look at me? It was making me insane. I didn't know why, but I wanted, needed her eyes on me, even though I knew I'd see only fear and disgust.

Walk away, now.

I should listen to the voice in my head but instead I strode across the room and sat in the seat closest to her.

Her gaze darted up to me from under her lashes, then back down. "Good evening, Constantine."

Her face was bright red and her voice shaky. Always so polite when she saw me, always so restrained and well behaved. But I knew if I offered her my vein now, instead of drinking it from the wineglass sitting in front of her, she'd detonate for me again, just as she had the first night. Yes, I wanted to feed her again, badly, but so far I'd resisted, letting blood for her instead, then giving it to Alice, my cook, to pour for her evening meal.

Her throat trembled and her gaze slid to the glass and back to her meal.

"Drink, Delphine," I said, the monster rising to the surface.

Her gaze shot to me. "Oh, I...I'm not really thirsty—"

"Why are you lying to me?" Twisted anticipation filled my gut as I reached for a piece of steak, nice and bloody, the way I liked it, and dropped it on my plate. Yes, I found I had an appetite right now.

Her lashes fluttered as she looked everywhere but at me. I could see her mind racing behind her downcast eyes, searching for an excuse, then she stilled, like a pretty little mannequin when she realized her only option was the truth. "I've never really fed in front of anyone before," she said.

"You fed in front of me the first night I brought you here. Drink."

Her blush deepened, and her lids fluttered as she nodded jerkily and reached for her glass, taking a sip of my blood.

My cock stiffened at the sight, and I almost groaned when a drop slid over her full lower lip and she licked it up. "Is your new room adequate?"

Her hands trembled. "Yes, thank you."

Get the fuck up and walk out.

But I couldn't do it. Being the monster I was, I enjoyed the sound of her racing heart, the quickening of her breath, her nervousness, her shy responses far too much. I willed her to fucking look at me. She did not. If I were a male like her stepfather, I could use this girl to destroy him. I could debauch and break her, like he had Samara—and I'll admit, I had contemplated it, briefly. My fingers curled into a fist. But I was nothing like that sadistic fuck, and no matter whose roof Delphine had lived under most of her life, I would never sink that low.

"How have you been sleeping?" I cut off a piece of steak and slid it between my teeth, chewing it slowly, watching my bride as she tried to gather her courage to look at me in return. "As good as you did the first night?"

"Um...yes."

"You're lying again." I shouldn't toy with her, but I couldn't seem to stop myself.

She gripped her cutlery tighter and swallowed hard. "Sorry, no...not as good as the first night," she quickly amended.

Look at me. I almost snarled the words out loud. "I'm not surprised, after the way you came for me that night, little one, you passed out." Her gaze flew to mine then, eyes wide, confusion clear in their depths, finally giving me what I wanted, what I'd goaded her into. Christ, so innocent. That look was a punch to the gut. "The pleasure you felt, Delphine, when you drank from me, when you rubbed your virgin pussy against me until you orgasmed...twice."

She froze completely. "I...I've never. I'm sorry if I... I don't know what happened to me..." She jammed her lips together.

Seeing that look on her face—I found I didn't enjoy tormenting and goading her quite so much. She didn't even know how her own body worked. Her mother should have at least shared with her what would happen, what to expect. "You don't need to apologize," I said, the uncharacteristic urge to reassure, surprising us both.

Her hands were still trembling, and she lowered her knife and fork and dropped her hands to her lap, hiding them from me, and finally found her courage. She looked up at me again, though still not meeting my eyes, not for long anyway.

Her cheeks were pink again, and her gaze slid to my throat and back up. "No, my behavior that night was unforgivably unladylike. I...I don't know what came over me. I understand why you've chosen not to feed me that way again." She licked her lips nervously. "I know I've disappointed you, but please, don't send me back. I'll stay out of your way, and if you'd prefer I feed from another completely, I understand. I'm sure I could find someone else to...to help me if need be."

Her words shocked the fuck out of me. I searched for what to say, and the longer I said nothing, the more she shrunk in on herself. I didn't like it. No, I fucking hated it. Delphine wasn't just an extension of her twisted stepfather. I'd realized it that first night, much to my fucking dismay. And the fear I saw in her eyes now, at the prospect of going back to him, made me wonder if perhaps his sadistic nature had gone beyond his dungeon and into his home. "You haven't disappointed me." My voice sounded harsher than I'd intended, but I had no idea how to ease a female's fears. Samara had very rarely shown emotion, especially fear. "What happened the first night, your response to what you felt, was normal, and I don't give a fuck about ladylike behavior."

She blinked up at me, eyes wide. "Oh."

"I haven't fed you from my vein again, Delphine, because I assumed you'd need time to get used to me," I lied. *Why the fuck did I care about this female's feelings?* I had no idea, but apparently, I did, and to the detriment of my own sanity, if my next words were anything to go by. "The next time you feed, you will come to me." The possessive snarl to my voice caught us both off guard. "And you sure as fuck will not drink from anyone else."

She licked her lips nervously. "Yes, Constantine."

Her voice was soft and sweet and lifted tingles all over me. My cock was unbearably hard now, and the urge to throw her over the table and fuck her, to claim my little virgin bride, was almost overwhelming.

I stood, and she jumped in surprise. I bit back another snarl at her reaction. "I have things to do," I said and walked out of the room.

And I ignored the monster roaring in my head to go back, to pick her up, and take her with me.

Five

DELPHINE

"Do you think I could cut some roses for my room?" I asked John.

John was the groundskeeper. He was friendly, and we'd been chatting for a while. It was so nice to have an easy conversation with someone.

"Of course, mistress." He handed me a small pair of shears.

The roses were stunning, their colors vibrant, their perfume sweet and heady. I wanted to bring some of that color inside to brighten Constantine's dark, moody décor.

I'd spent most of the day exploring the house and the grounds. When Alice brought my breakfast this morning, she'd suggested it, since it was my home now, so I had. The place was huge, and the gardens absolutely stunning.

Thankfully, it was overcast today, so I was able to venture outside and check out the gardens. Despite what humans thought, vampires could walk in the sun, but the younger we were, the more sensitive we were to it. I'd seen the rose gardens from my bedroom window, and I'd been desperate to take a closer look. Roses were my absolute favorite flowers. We'd had several beds at home, but they were nowhere near as stunning as the ones here.

I moved to the next rose bed and selected another one. There were so many different varieties, and colors, I didn't know where to go first. My heart felt full for the first time in a long time.

My mind wandered to Constantine. I was finding it hard to think of anything else, honestly. After our exchange in the dining room, he'd gone back to avoiding me, like he had been since the first morning I woke and found him at my door, staring down at me, fangs long and sharp, eyes glittering, face contorted. Before he'd snarled at me, then walked away. The male could be terrifying, but on some level, I knew he wouldn't hurt me. He hadn't that morning, or since, and he'd had plenty of opportunity.

When he'd looked at me that first morning, I could see he wanted something from me, it shone in his eyes, I *felt* it. But I had no idea what it could be. No wonder he'd been angry. I was failing at this and I didn't know how to fix it.

It didn't help that my mate made me so nervous I stuttered and stumbled over my words when I was around him. No wonder he avoided me. Though, since then, I didn't think he gave me much thought at all. Maybe that was a good thing? Out of sight, out of mind, wasn't that the saying? That's what I'd been thinking, anyway. Well, at least until he'd sat with me at the table and aimed his deep violet eyes my way.

When he'd said all those confusing things.

I felt like an idiot. So sheltered, so inexperienced in all things that I couldn't even hold a simple conversation with him, and I'd been in a constant state of terror that he was going to send me home. That couldn't happen. I'd run away and take my chances by myself if it came to that.

Clutching my roses, I said goodbye to John, and strode across the lawn toward the massive gothic-style stone mansion as dark and forbidding as the male who owned it.

My mind spun. How could I give him whatever he wanted, like mother told me to, if he wanted nothing from me? And how could I keep him satisfied and happy if I didn't know what that entailed? I felt utterly lost. Did he expect me to just know?

I walked through the main doors and upstairs. There was a decorative vase on one of the dressers in my room and I filled it with water, arranged the roses, and placed them by my bed.

I still had a few left that wouldn't fit. I chewed my lip. Constantine obviously liked roses, this was his house after all and there were rose beds everywhere. I'd stumbled across his room while I'd explored the house earlier, it was just down from mine. Yes, he was cold and intimidating, but he hadn't hurt me, and last night I think he might have actually been attempting to put me at ease, at least at the end of our conversation.

I appreciated his trying, even if it didn't entirely work. I needed to thank him, and like my mother said, it was my job to make him happy. How could sweet-smelling roses beside his bed not make him smile? They made me smile.

Mind made up and belly alight with nerves, I grabbed the drinking glass by my bed, filled it with water, and arranged the remaining roses into a pretty posy, then slipped into the hall and rushed down to Constantine's room. I tapped lightly on the door. No reply.

Maybe I could just slip in and put them by the bed, a surprise for when he returned to his room later.

I eased the door open and rushed across the room. His bed was a massive four-poster made of dark wood with a black velvet duvet and curtains. There was also a matching wooden dresser and bedside tables.

His scent was strong in here, rich and enticing, and I found myself breathing deeply. I liked the way Constantine smelled, a lot. A shiver slid through me when I thought about what happened when I'd fed from him. I'd never experienced anything like that before in my life. I thought I'd done something wrong, that I'd disgusted him with my reaction to his blood, that he'd been avoiding me, but he said my reaction was normal, that he was giving me time.

He wanted to feed me from his vein again, and I wanted to

repeat the experience, though my humiliation fired back to life at the very thought. Because there was no way he hadn't noticed the wetness between my thighs, smelled it. I don't know why it happened, or what it was, but I really hoped it didn't happen again.

I quickly set the roses on the side of the bed I assumed was his. There was a lamp and a phone charger there.

A door opened behind me and I spun around.

The bathroom door.

Constantine walked out—and I froze.

He wore only a towel draped around his hips and nothing else. His smooth, tattooed skin was still damp, his dark hair slicked back. His gaze slid over me, and his abdominal muscles clenched. "What are you doing in here?"

"I was just..." I glanced at the posy and back. He ran his fingers through his damp hair, and I struggled to find the right words. "I walked around the gardens and I...well, I picked some roses. I put some in my room and thought..."

His gaze slid to the flowers beside his bed, then back to me. His eyes were cold, blank. "You thought what?"

I clutched my hands together to stop them visibly shaking. His accent was stronger, it did that sometimes, usually when he was focused on me. "Well, I...I assumed you liked roses, since you grow them here, and I...I thought you might like some in here as well."

His expression didn't change. "You thought I'd like roses by my bed?"

The urge to run, to get away filled me. I took a step back. "I'm sorry. I shouldn't have assumed...they're just so pretty and they smelled so nice, I just thought..." I shook my head. "I'll leave you to dress." I turned and ran from the room, down the hall and into my own, slamming the door shut behind me.

I didn't know what the right thing to do was. I'd barely been around anyone, let alone a male like Constantine. I was out of my depth in every way. My face burned with humiliation. I'd been alone, lonely, for so long that I didn't know how to behave, what to do or say.

I didn't want to be alone anymore, but I was messing everything up.

~

I tossed and turned.

My mind kept replaying my humiliation over and over again. The way Constantine stood in front of me, bare chested and tattooed, skin damp, hair wet, a look on his face like—I'd lost my mind completely.

I groaned, my face heating again.

Shoving back the covers, I pulled on my robe and headed downstairs. Maybe a book would shut my mind up. I walked into the library and I'd found Alice sitting in one of the overstuffed chairs reading. There was a big, steaming mug and a plate of cookies on the small table beside her.

"Sorry, I didn't mean to interrupt," I said and took a step back, about to leave.

"Nonsense. Come in." She held out her plate of cookies. "I like to read down here before bed, I find this room relaxing."

I took one. "It is a nice room. I was just... I couldn't sleep. I thought a book might help."

"What are you in the mood for?"

I glanced around the large room. "I'm not sure."

"How about a romance? I have a whole collection of them over there, on the middle shelf."

"I wouldn't know where to begin."

Alice put her book aside and walked over scanning the colorful spines. "How about a handsome billionaire and his best friend's younger sister?"

I blinked down at the book she held out.

"It's one of my favorites," she said. "The heroine's had a crush on him for years and the hero finally pulls the stick out of his butt and makes a move when he sees her with someone else." She cackled. "The hero loses his mind over it. It's wonderful."

I'd never read a romance before, but I liked the sound of it. I also liked the idea of the female having the upper hand for once. That was never the case in my experience.

I thanked her, took it to my room and got back into bed. After the first page I was hooked. I'd devoured almost half the book before my eyes started to droop, and I kept reading the same paragraph over and over again. I put the book down and let my eyes drift shut.

When I woke again, light was peeking through the curtains. I stretched, pushing back the covers and got out of bed, drawing back the curtains. I really hoped we had another overcast day. I wanted to venture out to the gardens again. The sun was trying to fight its way through the low clouds. I'd duck out right after breakfast. Just in case.

I turned from the window, and stilled—there was a rose on the pillow beside mine.

Red and long stemmed. I hadn't picked any of the red ones yesterday, only pinks and yellows.

I looked around my room, as if the answer was there somewhere, but there was only one explanation, wasn't there?

Constantine.

It had to have been him.

But why would he have done that?

I quickly showered. Thankfully, my clothes had been loaded into Constantine's car by his people before we'd gone out to the garden, before Douglas had sent someone after us. I shoved all thought of him from my mind and opened my wardrobe.

Dresses mainly, all beautiful and no doubt costly. My mother had selected some new clothes for me, anticipating my entry into society and their own rise. She'd told me that I needed to look good at all times, that my mate would expect it.

The last thing I wanted to do was disappoint Constantine or embarrass him. I selected a sundress in a deep violet. It skimmed my upper body and flared out at my hips, hitting just above the knee. I slipped on silver sandals and spent time on my hair, added a touch of makeup, then headed downstairs.

Constantine wasn't in the dining room this morning, and he didn't join me. I forced myself to eat, but it was hard with my belly all fluttery and nervous. I heard footsteps and I sat up straighter, my insides doing a deep swoop.

Alice hustled around the corner, not Constantine, and I couldn't decide if I was relieved or disappointed. I stood when she started clearing the table. "Thank you, Alice, breakfast was delicious."

"You don't need to thank me," she said and gave me a wide grin, which told me she appreciated it all the same.

Because people liked to feel appreciated when they did nice things for others.

Like leave roses on their pillows.

Yes, I was still embarrassed over what happened last night, but Constantine had left a rose for me. The polite thing to do would be to thank him.

I thought about him coming into my room while I'd slept. What if my mouth was open? Or I was drooling, or talking in my sleep or snoring? Heat washed through me, a wave of embarrassment turning me pink from head to toe all over again.

I cringed, but straightened my spine and called on all the courage I possessed, and went in search of him. He wasn't hard to find. His scent filled this place, and the closer I got to him, the stronger his scent grew. My nose led me right to his office door.

Taking a fortifying breath, I knocked.

"Come in," he said roughly.

When I walked in, he was sitting behind his desk with what looked like maps and some other papers spread out in front of him. He looked shockingly fierce and...handsome sitting there with those strong features and the brutal scar down the side of his face. I'd never really thought about his looks, my fear had gotten in the way, but for some reason, it didn't now and I realized I...liked the way he looked. His midnight hair was combed back, and he was wearing a navy shirt. He'd rolled up the sleeves, and the collar was undone, revealing his tattooed skin. I had the sudden and strong urge to bury my face there, to breathe deeply, then sink my fangs into him.

"Do you need something, Delphine?"

I jumped at his harsh tone but refused to flee again. I straightened my spine and stepped deeper into the room. His dark gaze sliced down my body, then back up to my face, my hair. His expression remained unchanged, but his Adam's apple slid up and down his thick throat.

I brushed my hands over the skirt of my dress. "I'm sorry for the interruption, Constantine. I just wanted to say good morning and to..." I swallowed, my mouth dry all of a sudden. "The rose you left on my pillow; it was...it was lovely."

He said nothing, but those cold eyes were still focused on me.

Why wasn't he speaking? Was he waiting for me to do or say something more?

In the book I was reading, when the heroine's male did something nice, she kissed him. Was he waiting for me to do that? If I didn't show him that I wanted to be his friend, how would he know? And if he thought I didn't like him, he might send me back to my stepfather. I had to be brave. I had to show him I could be his friend, that I could be a good mate to him.

He was so tall and broad and intimidating, but I forced myself to walk across his office and round his desk. He followed me with those cold yet beautiful violet eyes, but he didn't move, didn't speak.

My knees felt wobbly when I stopped beside him. The male in the book had loved it when his female had shown him affection. I'd lived without it all my life, but remembering the way it felt pressed up against Constantine, when I fed from him, his hands gripping me close—yes, I'd liked it, and I wanted to feel that way again. I wanted it badly.

Constantine had to know I was afraid of him, and yes, I could admit I was, more than a little, so I had to show him I could be brave as well. So I took another step closer, leaned in, and pressed a kiss to his jaw, the only place I could reach.

He stilled even more.

"Thank you for my rose," I said and straightened.

I waited for him to say something, he didn't, but his fingers tightened around the pen he held, so tight his knuckles turned white.

Was he...angry? Oh god, he obviously didn't want affection from me. "I'll leave you to your work," I said, my face burning fiercely again. I forced myself to turn away and walk across the room at a reasonable pace, and not run like I was desperate to.

Don't cry. Do not cry.

I reached for the door.

"Delphine?"

I stopped in my tracks and turned back, my heart racing wildly in my chest. "Yes?"

"Your dress, you look...nice this morning."

Pleasure filled me, despite the slight growl to his voice. I ignored that and focused on what he'd said. "I'm glad you like it." I brushed my hands down my waist. "I chose it for you."

"Did you?"

I nodded. "My mother told me a female should always look nice for her mate."

He sat back in his seat. "Do you like the dress?"

I looked down at it, then back up. "Um...yes. It reminds me of your eyes."

He went motionless again. "I have work to do."

I didn't want to leave, but he obviously didn't want me to stay.

Hurt filled my chest, but I did my best to hide it. "Perhaps I'll see you later, then," I said and rushed out.

~

Constantine

I didn't want her to leave, which was why she needed to get the hell out.

She walked out of my office, her sundress clinging to her delicate frame, and I cursed. My skin still tingled where she'd pressed her soft, warm lips. My little bride was a lot braver than I thought, and utterly confounding. She was as scared as a frightened rabbit around me, but still she sought me out, she even kissed me, she'd spoken of my eyes.

I bit back a growl, my fingers curling into a fist. Why the fuck had I picked that damned rose? What had compelled me to do such a thing?

She'd run from my room last night, red-faced, unable to meet my eyes, and once again, I'd had the utterly foreign urge to ease her discomfort, to make the pain in her eyes go away. The next thing I knew I was in the garden selecting the perfect fucking bloom.

Her light had been on late into the night, and I'd paced past her door for hours. And when it finally went out and I was sure she was asleep, I'd snuck in—and like a fool, I'd lingered in her room far longer than I should have.

She'd been asleep on her back, looking so fucking fragile, I hadn't been able to leave. And I hadn't, not until the urge to pick her up and carry her to my bed became overwhelming.

What was wrong with me?

You planted those roses for her. And deep down it pleased you that she loved them, just like you'd once hoped she would.

I shoved my fingers through my hair and stood. "Fuck."

Striding from my office, I walked out the front door and got in my car. I needed to get away, just for a few hours. My house suddenly felt small, her scent, her presence filled every square inch. Christ, it was taking everything in me not to search Delphine out now, just so I could be close to her.

So I could touch her again.

Despite what some might believe, my brothers and I weren't completely emotionless. Close, but not completely; though, Nero might be the exception—and the more time I spent with Delphine, the more my muted emotions were being revived.

Morgan, the head of my security, rushed over as I strode to the garage. "Stay with my bride, no visitors, trust no one. Her stepfather is capable of anything."

Morgan strode back to the house and I got in my car.

Delphine was still young, she needed to feed more regularly than me. And going by the paleness of her eyes, it would need to be tonight.

And since I'd demanded she drink from me from now on, like a damned idiot, I needed to gather my control because if my little bride went as wild as she had the first time I fed her, I wasn't sure I'd be able to keep the monster leashed.

Six

DELPHINE

ALICE WINCED when I spilled cupcake mixture on the floor.

"Oh! I'm so sorry." I quickly wiped it up. "I promise I'll clean everything when I'm done."

"You don't need to do that, Mistress Caputo. That's my job."

"Please call me Delphine or Del." I liked the idea of that. Mistress Caputo sounded so weird and I'd never had a nickname. "And it's my mess, so I'll clean it."

She shook her head. "No, you will not. Mr. Caputo wouldn't like it."

Morgan, who I'd met for the first time today, sipped his coffee, a small grin curling his lips. I'd seen him about the place, but this was the first time we'd talked. He said he was head of security.

"You don't have to hang around here. Honestly, I'm fine," I said to him. I really didn't need an audience witnessing my terrible baking skills.

"Constantine told me to stay with you."

"He did?" I tossed the tea towel down on the counter. "Why? Where is he? Does he think there's some kind of danger?"

"I couldn't tell you where he is, he didn't say when he left. And we're just being cautious."

I nodded and got back to measuring batter. Despite Morgan's attempt to ease my fears, they remained. I was sheltered, yes, but not totally naive, not when it came to my stepfather, at least. Constantine had refused to pay my dowry for some reason, and Douglas would come after him again like he had in that garden. They obviously believed that as well.

I forced my stepfather from my mind and checked the recipe for the next ingredient. Chocolate chunks. I opened the bag and managed to tear it in half, causing chocolate to spill all over the counter.

"It's fine," Alice said before I could apologize again.

I tried to hide my embarrassment and gathered up what I could and dropped several on top of each cupcake. Alice opened the oven and I carried over the tray and slid them in. "The recipe says twenty minutes."

Alice smiled warmly and I smiled back. I'd never baked anything in my life, and the sense of accomplishment I felt was wonderful. I got to work cleaning, ignoring Alice's protests and Morgan's chuckles, and I enjoyed that too.

When the timer dinged, I rushed over and opened the oven—

"Wait, you need to—"

I pulled the tray out—"Ow!"—and dropped it when it burned my hand, my cupcakes falling to the floor.

Alice rushed over. "It's hot, Delphine, you need a cloth."

Of course, it was. I should have thought of that, but I'd been too excited. Alice grabbed my wrist and led me to the sink, turning on the cold water. Tears welled in my eyes. I'd made them for Constantine. The heroine in my new book owned a cupcake shop and the hero had a sweet tooth, and I knew Constantine still ate food, I'd seen him.

My mate might not have reacted the way I'd hoped when I left him roses, not at first, but then he'd left one on my pillow. His response to me showing him affection hadn't been that wonderful, either, but then he'd complimented me on the way I looked.

I realized after I'd visited him in his office that this was all new to him as well. He was an intense male, a warrior used to the battlefield; he needed time to adjust, like I did. And maybe his reaction to my cupcakes wouldn't be what I hoped for, either, not at first, but I was ready for that now.

I wanted to please him. I wanted kisses and hugs like I'd read about in my book. I wanted him to hold me like he had the first night I came here, and I couldn't have any of those things if I didn't make him happy, if I didn't please him.

How did you make someone like you? According to my book, the answer was cupcakes. And if he liked me, he'd be less likely to send be back.

My heart pounded as I stared at the ruined cakes, a panicky feeling filling me. "They're ruined. I need delicious cupcakes, Alice. I need them."

Alice patted my shoulder. "It's okay. We'll just make more."

I swiped the tear that embarrassingly streaked down my cheek and smiled. "Thank you."

I sat under a fluffy blanket in the library, trying to read while I waited for Constantine to come home.

It was hard to concentrate on my novel when my nerves were in a constant flurry in my belly. I tilted my head when I thought I heard the front door. I'd been doing that all night, but everything was silent.

Alice had gone to bed and Morgan had made himself scarce, though, I assumed he was in the house somewhere.

I read the same sentence for the tenth time and sighed. Maybe Constantine wasn't coming home? Maybe he'd be gone the whole night, maybe longer? But why would he do that? The thought had the constant nerves in my belly churning. Had my kiss truly made him angry, angry enough to leave? Then why did he compliment my dress? I was so confused. If he'd just come home, I could give him his cupcake. Sugary treats definitely made me happy, they made everyone happy. Hopefully, that included broody warriors.

I tried to focus on my book again.

But the words on the page went fuzzy and my eyes grew heavy. I tried to keep them open, I wanted to be awake when he got home. I had to stay awake...

"Delphine?"

I jolted, my eyes flying open. "You're here."

"Yes, I..."

I shoved off the blanket and jumped to my feet, wobbling for a moment in my haste, then snatched up the plate with the cupcake I'd made him. It was vanilla with chocolate frosting. "I made you this," I said and held it out.

He blinked down at it. "What is it?"

"A cupcake. I thought you might like a sugary treat. I wanted you to have something nice when you got home and..." He took one of my hands, lifting it.

"What is this?" he said, studying my palm.

"I burned it."

His dark violet eyes slid from my palm to my face. "How?"

I licked my suddenly dry lips. "I've never baked before, and I didn't think to use a cloth for the tray. It burned my hand, and I dropped the cupcakes all over the floor."

He looked at the cupcake I was holding and back at me.

"The first batch was destroyed. I started from scratch," I said quickly. "I would never give you floor cupcakes."

"You made a second batch?"

"Yes."

"After you burned yourself, so I could have a sweet treat?"

"Yes."

He looked at my palm again, his expression turning to stone. "You're still young, Delphine, you heal slowly, you need to be more careful."

It was already looking better than it had. I healed slower than an older vampire like him, but I still healed relatively quickly. I didn't say that though, not with that intense and, yes, angry expression on his face. My heart sank, but I made myself smile and nod.

His gaze went to my mouth and he swallowed thickly, then released my hand and took a step back. "You should head up to bed, it's late." He turned, about to leave.

"Your cupcake," I called after him.

"You have it." He walked out the door.

"Oh...okay." But he was already gone.

I stared after him, and before I could stop it, a sob escaped, surprising me. I covered my mouth with my hand to stifle the next and sat heavily.

I thought coming here meant my years of loneliness had finally come to an end. I'd been so incredibly wrong.

Constantine didn't want me, and it was only a matter of time before he sent me away.

Constantine

Her sob stopped me in my tracks.

I shoved my hands in my pockets and stared at the floor. *Fuck.* I turned back to the door, then willed myself to ignore her and walk away, but I couldn't do it.

"Fuck," I muttered and walked back into the library.

Delphine looked up, startled, like the night I'd brought her here. She swiped at the bloody tears on her cheeks and offered me that same fake smile, pretending she hadn't been in here crying just now despite the evidence.

"Give me the cake. I changed my mind," I said and sat on the couch beside her. She was in her nightgown. Simple, sensible white cotton, cotton that was far too fucking thin. Christ, I could see right through it. "I'm in the mood for a...a sweet treat," I gritted out.

Her smile widened, and this time it wasn't fake. "You are?"

I lifted the tiny cake from the plate and peeled back the red polka-dot paper that covered the base of it and took a bite.

"What do you think?" she asked, her expression hopeful.

It was terrible. "Is it supposed to be salty?"

"What? No!" She took it from me and bit into it. A wail of despair followed.

"Delphine?"

"It's horrible." She covered her face and another sob burst from her.

What the hell was going on? "It's not that bad," I lied.

She shook her head and didn't look up. "I used salt instead of sugar, Constantine. It's awful. God, I'm an idiot."

"It was just a mistake. Why are you so upset?" I asked, dumbfounded.

She dropped her hands, her face streaked with tears. "Because I want you to like me. It's always just been me and my maid, and she wasn't allowed to talk to me about anything other than her duties. I thought now that I'm free...that I'm here, that we could be..." She shook her head, her lips trembling as her pretty lavender eyes met mine. "That we could be friends."

Something inside me cracked down the middle. This was my fault, all of it. I'd always thought the practice of claiming your mate when they were still so young was barbaric, locking the female away until the male was ready to claim her, so fucking wrong. I'd vowed never to do it. Then I'd felt Delphine. I'd followed the feeling inside me, the connection to her, and it had taken me right to her.

There was no walking away after that.

But after what happened to Samara, then learning Douglas's connection to my mate, I'd stopped planning for the day I brought Delphine home. She had no longer factored. I hadn't allowed myself to think about her, or imagine what she was like. I certainly hadn't allowed myself to think about what this would do to her. She'd paid a price because of my hunger for revenge, not just her piece-of-shit stepfather.

I swiped the frosting from the cupcake and ate it. "This part's good. It's sweet."

She blinked rapidly. "Is it?"

I swiped more and held it up. I meant for her to take it from me, but before I knew what she was doing, she gripped my hand, wrapped her lips around the tip of my finger, and sucked it off. My cock, already hard just from being in the same room as her, stiffened to painful proportions. And all the while, those big eyes were on me, completely innocent to what she was doing to me.

"Oh, that is good." She licked her lips. "Do you like me?"

The sudden change of topic took me by surprise, and the desperation to her voice caused a weird pain in my sternum.

I didn't know what it was that this tiny female had done to me, but I couldn't find it in me to hurt her. "I like you just fine, little one."

"I like you too," she whispered.

What the hell was I going to do with her? This wasn't how it was supposed to be. I was supposed to be avoiding her—but I couldn't. And it was only a matter of time before I fed her again. How the hell would I keep my control then?

"You should go to bed," I said, because I was hard and achy and hungry for her and being alone with her right now was testing every bit of my restraint.

She didn't say anything for several seconds, reluctant to go, I fucking felt it.

"Will I see you in the morning?" she asked.

"Yes." How was it that this tiny female had made cracks in the dark armor I'd surrounded myself with in such a short time, and was finding ways to slip through?

She stood to leave—her stomach rumbled.

My hand shot out, wrapping around her wrist, stopping her, the action controlled by another part of me, the base, demonic part utterly focused on its female and her needs.

Feed your mate. The predator inside me, the male who felt the connection to this female, roared through my head, to bear the notion of her wanting for even a moment. "You're hungry."

Her cheeks turned pink and she nodded.

"Why didn't you tell me?"

"After this morning, when I..." She shook her head. "I wasn't sure you'd still want to."

Possessiveness tore through me. "And what would you have done instead?"

She lifted one of her thin shoulders and let it drop. "Perhaps ask Morgan or John or one of the other guards I've seen walking around outside?"

No, that wouldn't do, not at all. I tugged her closer, gripped her narrow hips, and lifted her onto my lap, the monster taking control now. "If you fed from any of them, little one, if they *let you* feed from them... I'd kill them in a heartbeat. I'd tear out their throats, bleed them, dismember them, then incinerate them, understand?"

Delphine's heart was thundering, her blood rushing through her veins as she stared at me in shock.

"Do you understand, Delphine?" I bit out, the bonded male in me needing her to say it. We might not be officially mated, but that didn't mean anything to that part of me.

"Y-yes, I understand."

She was trembling. I'd frightened her, but there was nothing I could do about that now. She needed to get used to the type of male I was, and better she sees the real me now. The last thing I needed was her forming any romantic ideas about me, ideas that would never come true.

Then her scent hit me. My little bride's pussy was wet. My cock surged, close to punching through the front of my fucking trousers.

She squirmed and tried to get off me. "I just...I need to..."

I gripped her hips, stopping her. "Where are you going?"

"I'm not hungry anymore," she said as her belly rumbled again.

She tried to pull away and I held her tighter, keeping her planted on my lap. "I scared you," I said, and the fact that I sounded so fucking demonic probably wasn't helping. "I'm capable of a lot of things, Delphine, but I will never hurt you."

Her gaze stayed downcast. "I'm not scared."

"No? Then what is it?" She still wouldn't look at me. "Delphine?"

"Please, Constantine, let me go," she whispered, a blush coloring her cheeks.

I took her chin in my hand and tilted her head back. "You need to feed."

She squirmed again, trying to close her legs, sitting awkwardly on my lap. "Are you in pain?" Though, I didn't sense it and I was positive I'd sense it if that's what it was.

She shook her head and tried to squirm away again.

My patience ran out, and I tugged her close, not giving her any room. "Enough."

She stilled.

Delphine needed to feed. I could still hear her stomach rumbling, and it was making me crazy. "Tell me what's going on? Why you're trying to get away from me?" I demanded.

She chewed her lip, her gaze everywhere but on me. "I can't say."

Her embarrassment was clear. "We're bonded, there should be nothing you can't tell me. I expect honesty, Delphine. I demand it." No, I hadn't earned that right, and I was taking advantage of her innocence, but I needed to know what was upsetting her, and I needed to know right the fuck now.

Her lips quivered and she nodded, looking miserable. "B-between my legs...it's..." She choked out a pained sound. "It's... damp and disgusting, and I don't know what's happening, and I'm trying not to...get it on you."

It was my turn to go utterly still. Every time this female spoke, she put another crack in my armor. I took it for granted that she knew these things, when she knew nothing, definitely not about this.

She made a pained sound and tried to pull away again.

I didn't let her move, not even an inch. "You're wet because you're aroused."

Her expression didn't change.

Jesus. "When you fed from me last time, you felt pleasure, yes?"

She nodded.

"What you experienced was an orgasm, you came. When you rubbed against me, it felt good and you got wet. Your body is designed that way. It's natural, normal, it's what's supposed to happen."

Her mouth opened, closed. "But why?"

"To ease the way for your mate to slide inside you." My cock throbbed hard. Christ, the more we talked like this, the harder I got.

"Ease what inside me?"

"His fingers," I said, withholding the truth from her.

"Where?"

She couldn't be serious. "You've never touched yourself?"

"It's forbidden."

I told myself that I was doing this for her as I took her smaller, soft hand in my large, scarred one and slid it up her thigh and under her nightgown. I tried to convince myself that I was teaching her what she needed to know, but I was full of shit. I wanted to touch her so fucking badly. She tried to pull her hand away, but I kept hold of it.

"There are no rules here, not when it comes to this. You can touch your body any way you like." I pressed our joined fingers against her pussy. Fuck, I swallowed my groan. She was so incredibly wet, so hot. "You feel that?"

"Yes."

"That's your body readying for pleasure."

I pressed her finger to her slick folds. "You can explore this part of yourself, touch it, but especially here." I grazed her fingers over her clit, making her gasp. "Or here," I said and slid the top of her finger to her opening.

Her eyes widened and she shifted on top of me. "But it feels, it feels so small."

"You're made to stretch, and that will feel good as well." Why the fuck was I telling her this? I'd never planned to fuck her, to make her my mate in truth, being blood bonded to her was causing me enough trouble, but now I was just torturing myself.

She shook her head. "No, it won't fit."

"Push your finger inside."

"Constantine—"

"Do it," I ordered and applied pressure to her finger. It slipped in a little and she gasped. "Carefully, slide it deeper."

She did and I almost came. Her mouth fell open and she let out a desperate sound.

"Feels good?"

"Y-yes."

"Slide it almost all the way out, then back in. Do it."

She did. "Oh…"

"Again," I growled, losing my goddamn mind.

She did as I said, moving her finger in and out of her tight body.

"Faster, Delphine." I gathered her wetness and slid my thumb over her clit at the same time. She gasped and cried out, her hips starting to rock all on their own. "Do you feel it building?"

"I think...yes, I'm going to...I'm..." She arched, her breasts pressing against the cotton of her thin nightgown, her nipples tight and wanting.

I couldn't stop myself from leaning forward and sucking one through the cotton, teasing it with my tongue. I wanted to bite so badly my fangs slid down in anticipation.

She jolted in my arms and her head fell back a moment before she cried out, coming around her finger. I lifted my head and fisted her hair, holding her head up so I could watch. "That's it, let go. Come for me."

Finally, she collapsed forward, her face nestled against my throat. She panted, trembling as she nuzzled the pulsing vein there. "Bite," I demanded.

She did. She sank her fangs into my throat, her nails sinking into my skin and latching on as she drank and whimpered, rocking her hips again as another surge of need hit her with the taste of my blood.

"Do you want my fingers, little one?" Was that my voice?

She whimpered again and nodded as she drew deeply on my vein.

I gathered up her juices to ease the way, then covered her opening and carefully pushed inside. My finger was a lot bigger than hers, and she gasped but spread her thighs wider, silently asking for more. I pushed deeper, groaning at how tight and hot she felt as waves of hunger pounded over me with every pull she took on my vein.

She started rocking faster against my hand, fucking my finger, and I wasn't sure how I did it, but I managed to stop myself from throwing her down, tearing my pants open, and claiming her when everything inside me roared for me to do it. I slid deeper, working her inside, rubbing over the spot that would make her come hard, giving her the pleasure she'd been denied for far too long.

When she pulled away with a scream and came again, around my finger this time, her tight pussy soaking my hand.

She collapsed against me again, making small contented sounds that slid through my chest, settling in. She took several more lazy pulls on my vein, then licked, sealing it. Then she went limp, her breathing growing heavy.

She'd passed out on me.

I sat there, hard as fuck, not sure what the hell to do.

It was a long time before I finally stood and carried her to her bed.

And even longer before I dragged myself from her room and went to mine.

Seven

DELPHINE

I LOOKED at myself in the mirror. The gown I selected was deep blue with a fitted bodice and a flowing skirt. I ran my hands over the soft fabric as I took in my reflection. Alice had helped me with my hair and makeup, and I was wearing my silver sandals again.

There was a knock at the door. "You ready?" Constantine called.

Nerves zipped around in my belly. He was meeting with a couple of his brothers tonight, and they were bringing their brides. I really wanted to make a good impression.

The door opened. "Delphine?"

I turned.

Constantine stood in the door, wearing a dark suit that clung to his muscled body. The dress shirt he wore underneath was open at the throat and he was freshly shaven. His gaze traveled over me, slowly. He said nothing.

I ran my hands down my sides, my nerves growing even more. "Do I look okay?"

"You look beautiful."

Warmth filled me.

He held his arm out.

"Do you think the other females will like me?" I asked as I took it, unable to keep my fears in any longer.

"Yes," he said, and led me down the stairs.

"How do you know?"

"I just do."

We walked out to the car and Morgan and another male sat in the front. We got in the back and I tried not to fidget as we headed into the city.

"You're nervous," Constantine said beside me.

"I've never done anything like this before. You won't leave me alone, will you?"

He studied me for several seconds, a muscle in his jaw jumping. "No, I won't leave you alone."

His voice, that accent, rolled over me and set off little tingles across my skin. When I first saw him, I found him terrifying. I didn't anymore. He was fierce, yes, but also kind in his own way. And I liked his face. He was all angles and darkness and scars, but that suited him. Who gave him that scar? I assumed he got it during battle. Maybe the same time his heart stopped beating? Vampires usually healed completely, no matter the injury, but his injuries hadn't for some reason, permanently marking his skin. He had all those warrior tattoos as well. I liked those too. Seeing his inked hand with mine last night as he'd slid our linked fingers up my thigh—a shiver slid through me—had been mesmerizing.

"What are you thinking?" he said, startling me from my musings.

"Nothing," I said quickly.

His gaze locked on mine, so impossibly intense. "That was the wrong answer, Delphine."

"What do you mean—"

"You're lying to me."

Another shiver slid through me, but not from fear. From his voice, the way he looked at me, the way he said *Delphine* in that deep, rough way. He said there should be nothing I couldn't tell him. "How do you know I'm lying?"

He flashed his teeth. "It's all there in those pretty eyes of yours."

My pulse picked up speed. "Do I really have to tell you?"

"Yes."

Butterflies gathered in my belly. "I was wondering how you got the scar on your face." And before I knew what I was going to do, I touched his cheek with the tip of my finger and traced it down to his jaw. "And what happened to make your heart stop beating?"

He watched me, perfectly still. I quickly snatched my hand back, not sure what came over me.

"A fae blade," he said. "The steel they forge in their territory is the only thing that renders us as good as mortal."

I stared at him stunned. To survive a war like that, against weapons that could have killed him, he must be an incredibly skilled warrior. "I had no idea."

"As for my heart, I was a prisoner, held by the fae for some weeks."

"And they hurt you badly?"

He dipped his chin. "Then I slaughtered them and escaped. What else?"

I blinked, still processing what he'd just said. "Pardon?"

"What else were you thinking?"

I took a fortifying breath. "I was thinking how I love your accent, and how I was afraid of you the first night we met and, now, not so much. And that I like your face and your warrior tattoos, and I even like those things when you're being surly. That got me thinking about the things we did in the library and how much I enjoyed it, and that I'd like to do it again."

His nostrils flared.

The car pulled to a stop, and we were engulfed in silence.

"Constantine?"

He reached for me—

Someone opened his door and he muttered a curse. His gaze lingered on me for several beats, then he cursed again and climbed out, came around, and opened my door.

"Are you all right?" He seemed agitated.

His gaze dipped to my mouth and back up. "I've been better."

"Is there anything I can do to help?"

The violet of his eyes deepened. "Yes, but not while we're here. Let's go."

I wanted to ask how, but he still seemed tense, so I didn't push. I took his outstretched hand, and looked up at the house. "Who lives here?"

"This is Rainer's home."

"And just two of your brothers will be here?"

"Yes."

He called them brother because of their strong friendship and not because they were actual brothers. I knew this because I'd asked him. He led me up the stairs and the door opened before we reached it. We walked in, and the older male who opened the door motioned us to another door to the right.

My nerves fluttered wildly back to life as Constantine led me into the room.

Two massive males stood by a bar, talking low. Their brides sat on a couch on the other side of the room, huddled together in conversation. Both stood when I walked in. I remembered them both from the ceremony.

"Join the females," Constantine said and ushered me in their direction. "I need to talk with my brothers."

"You said you wouldn't leave me alone," I whispered desperately.

"I won't. I'll be right here in this room."

I wanted to plaster myself to his side, but that wasn't an option, so I took another breath to steady my nerves. "Okay."

He walked away, and I turned to the females watching me and forced myself to walk over to them. "Hello, I'm Delphine."

"I'm Ana."

"I'm Lucinda."

Ana had black hair, soft features, and her eyes were a vibrant lilac. Lucinda had long, wild red hair, lavender eyes, and a dusting of freckles across her nose.

"It's lovely to meet you both," I said.

Ana grabbed my hand and tugged me down to sit with her. "Are you okay?" She looked around me to Constantine.

Lucinda grabbed my other hand. "Has he hurt you?"

"No, he's been...good to me. And your males?"

Lucinda glanced across the room, then back. "No, Rainer hasn't hurt me. He's intense and quiet and looks at me like he wants to do...well, I don't know what, to me, but he hasn't hurt me."

Ana's face reddened. "Stefan likes me to drink from him, a lot."

"I think Constantine does as well," I said. "I know I do."

Ana grinned. "I, um, quite like it as well."

"How do you think the others are doing? Do you think we'll get to meet them?" Ana asked.

Lucinda sipped her drink. "I hope so. Maybe all of us could be...friends?"

"I'd like that," I said, a rush of happiness filling me. I hadn't sat down with females my age and had a conversation since I was fifteen years old and then only rarely.

Lucinda bit her lip. "Have you mated yet?"

"I don't know. I don't think so," Ana said.

"Oh, you'll know." Lucinda leaned in. "Rainer said we were bonded through the sharing of blood, but there's something else we have to do to become mated."

I straightened. "We're not mated yet?"

She shook her head. "There's something else."

"Did he say what we have to do?"

"No, but I don't think I'm going to like it. The other night I got angry with Rainer. I do all the talking and he says nothing, just clenches his jaw all the time. So I did the same and stopped talking, refusing when he demanded I speak again."

Ana's eyes widened. "What did he say?"

"He said he should just throw me over his desk and *take me*, just mate and get it over with before he loses his damned mind," she said, dropping her voice an octave lower, in an imitation of Rainer, I assumed.

"What does that even mean? Take you?"

She tucked her hair behind her ear. "I don't know, but he spent hours in the pool swimming lengths after that. So I put on my bathing suit and went to say sorry, and he growled..." She leaned in. "Then kissed me."

My belly flipped. "He kissed you?"

"Yes."

"Have you kissed Stefan?" I asked Ana.

Ana nodded, a shy smile curling her lips. "Has Constantine kissed you yet?"

I shook my head. "Not yet. What's it like? Did you...like it?"

"Oh yes," Ana said. "It was lovely."

"I'm happy to just stick with kissing. I'm not interested in whatever *taking me* entails," Lucinda said.

"Lucinda," a male voice growled out.

Her eyes went wide. Rainer stood behind us. None of us had heard him approach. Males as old as they were could move impossibly quick and utterly silent. He held out his hand.

"Are we going somewhere?" Lucinda asked.

"Yes," he said, and his voice sounded like Constantine's often did, all deep and rough.

She stood and took his hand, and he led her from the room.

I stayed with Ana and talked. Constantine and Stefan seemed deep in conversation.

When Lucinda finally returned, she was flushed, and she didn't come back to us right away. Rainer kept her by his side.

"Do you think she's okay?" Ana asked.

"I don't know. She doesn't look upset." Her lips were all puffy, her dress was rumpled, and her hair was disheveled. "She's smiling."

We stayed at Rainer's house for several more hours, and when Lucinda finally came back to us, she told us Rainer had taken her upstairs and thoroughly kissed her. I think there was more, but she didn't say, and I wondered if he touched her like Constantine had touched me while I fed last night.

When we were heading home, Constantine shifted in his seat, his focus coming to me. "Did you enjoy yourself?"

"I did."

"Did you like talking to the other females?"

"Yes, is that why you took me with you?"

"One of the reasons."

He didn't say what the other reasons were, and I didn't ask. All I cared about was that I had friends, for the first time in my life. "Will we get to meet the others?"

"In time."

I smiled, and he studied my mouth as I did. I couldn't help but admire his in return. Constantine had very nice lips. What would it be like to be kissed by him? The way Lucinda and Ana described it, it sounded like something I'd enjoy.

"What did you talk to Ana and Lucinda about?" he asked, one of his thick fingers tapping against his knee. He seemed distracted.

Sticking with my agreement to share and not keep things from him, I told him. "Our hobbies and our new situations, and how happy we were that none of our mates have been cruel to us. I shared how nice everyone at your home has been to me, and I told them about the lovely rose gardens you have. Oh, and kissing. Stefan seems to like kissing Ana, and Rainer's kissed Lucinda, a lot. He also said something about *taking her*, that's the way he said it apparently, *taking*," I said imitating the deep voice Lucinda had used. "And that he should just get the mating thing over with.

What does that mean? I thought we were already mated, but obviously not. What does *taking* entail? And do you think you'll kiss me? I think it sounds nice."

He stared at me for a long moment.

"Constantine?"

"Christ," he muttered and stared out the window. His fingers curled into a tight fist.

"Constantine?"

He said nothing.

My stomach sank. I wanted to be kissed so badly. "Do you not want to kiss me?" I bit my lip. "I shouldn't have asked, should I? It's probably not something everyone enjoys. I wouldn't know, I've never been kissed, but if you think we shouldn't do that, then I won't ask again." He squeezed the bridge of his nose. "You probably have to find the other person's mouth appealing to enjoy it? I like yours, but it's...it's okay if you don't like mine. My lips are a bit big, my lower one especially. Douglas said I had a whore's mouth, whatever that means. Do you think I have a whore's mouth? Constantine?"

He grabbed me so fast, I didn't see him move. One moment I was sitting beside him, the next I was on his lap. His fingers delved into my hair, cupping my head in one of his big hands, and he pulled my face down to his, our lips were barely an inch apart.

"No, you don't have a whore's mouth. You have a fucking gorgeous mouth, and I wanted to kiss you the moment I saw you. And yes, I'm going to kiss you, right now as a matter of fact, to stop you from talking, because if you keep talking, and saying the things you are, I will show you right here and now, what *taking* entails."

Then he pulled my face closer and pressed his lips to mine.

They were firm and warm. Oh yes, this was nice, really nice, then he rubbed them against mine and I enjoyed it even more. Each brush of his lips sent tingles racing all over my flesh. His grip grew firmer, and he kissed me more fiercely. It was confusing and exciting, and when he nipped my lower lip, they parted on a surprised cry.

Constantine's tongue darted out, licking at my lips, and I gasped. Did I like that? He did it again. Oh, I did. I did like it. He took my chin between his thumb and finger and opened my mouth, then swiped his tongue inside. My arms banded around his neck, holding him to me, and I touched my tongue to his experimentally. He growled and angled his mouth over mine, our tongues sliding against each other. I liked the way he tasted. Tingles started between my thighs, and I squirmed to get closer—

He suddenly pulled away with another growl.

I opened my mouth to protest, but he pressed his lips to mine again once, twice, without his tongue this time, then used his hand at the back of my head to press the side of my face to his chest.

"Well?" he asked after several seconds. "What did you think?"

He sounded strange. I tried to lift my head to look at him, but he held me firm where I was. "I really liked it. I hope we do it again." Again, I tried to lift my head, and again he kept me where I was. "Constantine?"

"Go to sleep, you must be tired."

"I'm not tired." I tried to lift my head again and this time he let me. "Lucinda said Rainer is going to *take her* tonight. Can you show me what *taking* entails when we get home?"

He closed his eyes and cursed under his breath.

"What?"

"We'll talk about it later."

"If you say so."

"I do."

"Can we do what we did in the library later, then? I'm feeling all tingly and wet, like I do when I feed. I think it has something to do with the kissing."

Constantine growled a third time but said nothing. His jaw was tight and his fingers were back to being curled into a fist.

Why wasn't he answering me? "Constantine?"

"Yes, Delphine?" he said, his voice so deep and odd it made me shiver.

"Did you hear what I said?"

"I heard you."

"Why do you sound like that?"

The car stopped and Constantine shoved the door open before Morgan could open it for him, taking me with him, and carried me toward the house.

"Constantine?" His gaze was focused straight ahead. "Are you going to touch me again?"

"Fuck, yes," he said and slammed his mouth down on mine again as we walked through the door and headed upstairs.

Eight

CONSTANTINE

I TOOK the stairs two at a time, my little bride wrapped around me. I wasn't supposed to be doing this, this wasn't the plan. But I wasn't strong enough to say no, not when she so innocently said the things she'd just said.

She wasn't ready to be fucked, no matter how wet she was. But I could touch her again. I could make her come for me over and over again. I'd go insane if I didn't.

This time her need didn't come about from feeding, no, this time she just craved pleasure, and wanted me to give it to her, badly. The monster would tear the fucking walls down if I didn't.

After talking to Rainer and Stefan, I knew my brothers were struggling as well. We might be cold and ruthless, but nothing had prepared us for this, for these innocent, bewildering, maddening, fucking mesmerizing females. I fisted Delphine's hair and kissed her more deeply. Her tongue tentatively touched mine again, and I was fucking lost.

I stormed down the hall to my bedroom door and kicked it open. The last couple of weeks had been torture with her just in the next room. Imagining her lying there all alone, so close, but not allowing myself to go to her.

Striding to the bed, I laid her across it, coming down on top of her. Her small body molded to mine. I was a big male, like my brothers, one of the biggest of our race, and Delphine was petite even by human standards, all the females at the ceremony had been. I had to be careful with her. Even if I wanted to fuck her now, I couldn't. She'd need to be prepared first, eased into it. But mating her wasn't the plan. I couldn't make her mine, and I had to resist it with everything in me.

For my sake, and for Delphine's.

Nothing had changed. I was going to kill Douglas, a male she'd grown up with, who was like a father to her. Making her mine was pointless because she'd want nothing to do with me after I killed that fucker. I'd had to make a choice, claiming my mate or avenging Samara.

As desperately as I craved the little female under me, I couldn't let Douglas get away with what he'd done.

Delphine didn't know any different. Didn't know what sex was, or what it entailed, and I didn't plan on enlightening her. Gathering up her gown, I pushed it higher, and the scent of her slick pussy intensified. I rolled her to her side, slid down the zipper of her gown, and tugged it below her shoulders.

"Constantine...what are you doing?"

"I'm going to pleasure you, little one," I said. "You want that, don't you?"

"Yes...yes, I want it. But why are you taking off my dress? I just want you to touch me between my legs."

Jesus, so damn innocent? "Let me show you."

I dragged her dress off and bit out a curse at the sight of her. The gentle mounds of her breasts wrapped in lace, the curve of her hips, the softness of her thighs, the way her damp panties clung to her delicate slit, making my mouth water to taste her.

Instead, I kissed her again, and she wrapped her arms around me, those pointed nails of hers scoring my back as she squirmed beneath me, wrapping her thighs around my waist on instinct alone.

My hips surged forward, and I growled when the hard length of my cock brushed over her hot pussy. Somehow, I fought the impulse to tear her underwear off and impale her on my cock, and instead kissed my way down her slender throat. But fighting how much I wanted her was only made harder by the fact that this female was made for me. Everything about her drew me in, that was just how it was. Her scent, her voice, the shape of her body, the color of her hair, and though she hadn't seen it at first through her fear, it was the same for her. Everything about me was made to entice her.

How the fuck was I going to fight this?

I shoved the thought from my mind and focused on pleasuring my bride. Undoing her bra, I tugged it down her arms and revealed her soft breasts and peach-colored nipples. They were small and tight, and I sucked one into my mouth with a groan. Delphine cried out, her fingers thrusting into my hair as she wriggled and rocked against me. I grabbed her hip with one hand to still her, anymore friction and I'd disgrace myself. Something I hadn't done since I first discovered what my cock could do.

I was known for my control, for my ability to please a female, to hold my own release back until she was sweaty and spent and shaking, and now this beautiful, naive, little female had me close to coming in my trousers and I'd only sucked her nipples.

She grabbed at my shirt when I sucked more firmly, pinching and teasing the other at the same time. The sound of fabric rending filled the room. She was still learning her own strength. After feeding from me, all she was meant to be was starting to be realized. She'd torn my shirt right down the back. I lifted and tugged it off, and she took in my upper body with hungry eyes, her hands sliding over my chest, my abdominals, the warrior tattoos covering my skin.

The look in her eyes had my stomach trembling and my fucking hands shaking. It was too much. I fell on her again and sucked and kissed my way down her ribs, over her belly.

"Constantine!" She shoved at my head. "What are you doing, you can't mean to—"

I shoved her thighs wide and opened my mouth over her pussy and those soaked panties. Forcing her slit open with my tongue right over the lace. She went from shoving me away to fisting my hair with both hands and pushing me back down.

I chuckled darkly. "You like that?"

"Oh...yes, I like it. Please, Constantine, don't stop."

There was no chance of that. Gripping the sides of her panties, I tugged them down her legs and tossed them on the floor. *Fuck me.* She lay there, perfect, willing, desperate for more. My cock was a hot rod of molten steel, but somehow I ignored the pounding need to fuck and fell back between her thighs, throwing them over my shoulders and covering her pretty pussy with my mouth again.

She cried out, lifting her hips, twisting, thrashing as I lapped her up, toying with her clit, teasing her tight opening with the tip of my tongue. I knew what she wanted, and I would give it to her, but I wanted to make her come with only my tongue first.

Seconds later she rewarded me with a high-pitched scream, and I licked her up greedily. She collapsed back, her small frame trembling hard. I stayed where I was, easing my licks but not stopping.

"Nothing to say now, Delphine?"

"Umnh?"

I laughed again. I finally knew how to stop all her questions, most of them ones I couldn't answer. But I got the feeling she had a lot more up her sleeve, more I wouldn't be able to give her answers to.

I kissed her inner thigh. "More?"

Her hips rolled, and the sound she made was between a gasp and a sob. "Y-yes...please."

Christ, she was going to kill me with the desire she had burning through me, scorching through my veins, tearing at my gut. I fucking ached for her in a way I never had for anyone else.

Delphine whimpered, and the monster, the bonded male could do nothing but answer, desperate to ease my female.

I lapped at her stiff clit and rubbed my thumb over her opening. "You want me to push inside, Delphine?"

She whimpered again. "Yes, do it."

I rubbed over her opening again, then slid my finger inside as I gently sucked her oversensitive clit. Her cry ripped through me as she shifted restlessly, wanting more, needing it but not sure how to ask for it. I slid in deep and back out, over and over again, working her higher without allowing her to tip over to oblivion. She sobbed and rocked and thrashed. I should let her come, and even though I tried to deny it to myself, I knew what I was doing—preparing her for more.

More that she will never get from you.

I snarled, my inner voice fighting with the desire burning through me. Desire won, and I slipped in a second finger, stretching her wider, because that's what I'd do if I was going to make her my mate. I'd make her come like this every night, getting her relaxed, used to me, giving her more, easing her up to three fingers until she was stretched out enough to take my cock, and even then, it would be a tight fit.

The mental images filling my head were a torment, and I pressed my cock hard against the covers as I fucked her with my fingers, the sound of her cries, how wet she was, her scent almost breaking me. Hunger hammered through me, so intense there was no fighting it anymore. I had to take something, or I'd shatter. I'd become the monster, the relentless warrior, and I wouldn't just take her, I'd take all of her.

So I did the only thing I could, I shoved my fingers deep inside her and bit down on the tender flesh surrounding her clit. Delphine shrieked, her pussy bearing down on my fingers so tight there was no pulling them free, spasming over and over as she came hard, soaking my fingers, jerking and trembling, and sobbing, calling my name.

I lapped up her blood and come and my fucking eyes rolled into the back of my head from the pleasure of it. My balls tightened and I was moments from coming all over myself, and it took all of my self-control to stop it.

Delphine collapsed back, one final sob bursting from her, the sound squeezing something behind my ribs. She jolted as I licked her again gently, sealing my bite, healing it, then kissed my way back up her body. I looked down at her. Her eyes were closed and her breathing was faster than it usually was when she slept.

My bride had passed out again from pleasure.

I stared down at her for several more minutes, trying to decide what to do. I should carry her back to her own bed, but I found I didn't want to. Now that I'd decided to enjoy her this way, I wanted her here with me, available to me. I wanted my talkative bride beside me.

You're playing a dangerous game. This is a mistake.

Maybe, but I couldn't stop, not now. She'd just come, screaming my name, in my bed. I still had the taste of her, of her pussy, of her blood on my tongue. The bonded male wouldn't let her leave, not now.

But I had it under control.

If I felt myself slipping, all I had to do was think about her sadistic stepfather, about Samara, and I'd find the will to resist. Because despite who she was and the reasons I couldn't mate her, she was still mine, my reward for centuries of war, of blood and violence and death. She was the softness I'd been without for so long.

So I was going to keep her with me, and I was going to enjoy her until I didn't crave her any longer. Until my hunger for her eased—and I could bring myself to walk away.

Because softness was never meant for me.

I was a warrior.

Eventually, I would have to return to that life.

The alternative was a fantasy, and something I couldn't allow myself to even contemplate.

Nine

DELPHINE

I walked through the garden, admiring the roses and breathing in their perfume. I'd been able to venture out here the last two days because the sun had thankfully stayed firmly behind the clouds.

I loved it out here. Music drifted from somewhere in the garden, though it was the kind of music Douglas had forbidden me from listening to. I followed it, rounding one of the larger rose beds, and found John. He was pulling weeds, the music coming from a cylinder-shaped device nearby.

"Good afternoon, John."

He jolted and looked up. "Mistress, I didn't see you there."

"Sorry if I startled you. I heard your music and couldn't help but follow it."

"I shouldn't have had it so loud. I can turn it off. I don't want to disturb your walk." He reached for it.

"No, please, leave it. I like it." It was upbeat and made me want to move.

He smiled. "My work seems to go a lot quicker when I'm listening to my favorite songs."

"Do you dance to it?" I asked.

He chuckled. "I'm not much of a dancer."

"Me either. I'm afraid I'm not very good at it. It wasn't something I was permitted to do."

He stood, brushing his dirt-streaked hands on his jeans. "That's a crying shame, mistress."

"Please, call me Delphine, or Del. Mistress makes me feel, I don't know, odd."

"If that's what you'd prefer." He grinned. "And dancing's as easy as moving to the music, I believe. There's no right or wrong."

The next song started. It was a little faster, and I did as John said and let the melody wash over me and began to sway. "Like this?"

He nodded. "Yeah, just like that."

I lifted my arms with a laugh and tilted back my head, reveling in the warm breeze and the wonderful music filling the rose garden, so happy in that moment I couldn't contain it. "What about this?" I asked.

He chuckled. "That's good as well."

I spun around, laughing and moving my hips and throwing out my arms, letting my body take over as a feeling of freedom, the kind I'd never known before, filled me. It was marvelous.

I opened my eyes and John was studying me.

"Am I doing something wrong?"

He shook his head. "If you're enjoying it, how can it be wrong?"

I smiled wide. "Dance with me?"

"I'm not sure that's a good idea."

"Please?"

"Like I said, I'm not much of a dancer."

I held out my hands. "We'll figure it out together."

He rubbed his dirt-stained hands on his pants again and took mine with a laugh. "What do you think we should do now?"

I thought about the way Constantine and I danced at the ceremony. "Put one of your hands on my shoulder and the other on my waist, it'll be easier to move together."

He did as I suggested and we began to sway together.

"How's that?" John asked.

"Yes, just like that. This is fun." I did prefer dancing with Constantine, though.

The song ended, and we carried on dancing to the next one when it started, slower this time. "Thank you for this, John. Do you think...we could be friends?"

"I'd be honored." His expression grew more serious. "Though, I'm not sure Constantine would like it."

"You don't?"

"Males are possessive of their mates, Del."

"Oh, we're not mated. I thought we were, but there's something we have to do before that happens. Though, I'm not sure what it is."

"You're not?"

I shook my head. "We're blood bonded, but that's all."

"Do you want to become his mate?"

I thought about it. I never had before, it was always just a fact that whoever came for me the night of the blood moon ceremony was who I'd be mated to. I'd never had a choice, so I'd never allowed myself to consider it. "I think so. He can be grouchy and bossy and intense, but he's never cruel." He was also very handsome, and the way he touched me... I barely suppressed my shiver.

"Wouldn't you rather be mated to someone who makes you happy? Someone who isn't grouchy or bossy? Someone who dances with you and laughs with you? Wouldn't you prefer that?"

A weird feeling gripped me at the things he said, and it was unpleasant, because I did want those things, badly. "I don't think I want to talk about this anymore. I'm not sure I should."

"Of course. I'm sorry if I offended you. But I do want to be your friend. I'm here if you ever want to talk. I know this must be hard for you, especially after how sheltered you must have been."

My face heated. "You didn't offend me."

His hand remained loose at my waist. "Where's Mr. Caputo now? Why isn't he with you?"

"He had to meet with some of his brothers."

John nodded. "I expect he'll be leaving again soon."

My heart gripped. "Leaving?"

"He's a warrior, Del. The commander of The Five, a protector of our race. He's never here long before he's back out patrolling the borders of our territory. The war might be over, but they'll need to remain vigilant, and a warrior like him won't be satisfied stuck in one place, under one roof when he's used to sleeping under the stars. The fighting and the blood, it's part of him."

Constantine was going to leave? He was going to leave me? I was going to be all alone again? I couldn't bear to think about it. "I need to go."

"You're upset?"

"No, I'm fine."

"I shouldn't have said anything." He kept swaying to the music. "My cottage is just over there." He motioned to it on the other side of the garden. "I feel bad that I upset you. I could make us tea, we could talk some more, as friends," he said.

"I'm not... I don't know if I should."

"I messed everything up, didn't I?" he said, his mouth twisting to the side. "I'll let you get back to your walk."

"No, you didn't. It's just, well, I'm not sure Constantine would like it."

John stepped back. "Look, I respect Mr. Caputo, a lot. But you need to stand up for yourself. You can't let him control you. Males like that will run right over you if you give them the chance. If you want a life of your own, you need to look out for yourself, and yes, make time for friends, or it'll be very lonely for you when he's not here."

I was going to lose Constantine. He was going to leave, and if I wasn't careful, I'd be without friends as well. The thought of being here alone, with no one to talk to, sent jagged fear through me. "I'd love to have tea with you sometime."

John smiled.

We swayed faster, then John spun me. When he pulled me back, my front collided with his. We both laughed.

"Delphine," a rough male voice called across the garden.

Constantine.

Pleasure instantly filled me. He'd only been gone for a matter of hours and I'd missed him. How would I stand it here alone if he was gone for months?

John's gaze went to Constantine and he stilled. "I'm not sure you should tell him we're friends, he'll be angry, Del—with me and with you."

I blinked up at him confused. "No, he won't be—"

"He will."

I pulled away from him, and turned to Constantine, and there was no containing my smile at the sight of him. He was striding across the garden—his expression like thunder. My smile slipped.

Constantine growled at John. "Why the fuck were you touching my female?"

John went pale. "She asked me to dance with her, Mr. Caputo. That's all it was. I didn't like to say no."

He'd enjoyed our dancing. I knew he did. John was lying because he was right, Constantine was angry. I could see it in the way he held himself, and I thought he might actually hurt the smaller male.

I stepped forward, into the path of Constantine's fury, pressing my hands to his chest. "I just wanted to dance, that's all. I didn't know it'd make you angry. It's not John's fault, it's mine."

His fingers were clenched in tight fists, and his rage-filled gaze was still locked on John.

"Please, I'm sorry," John said. "I didn't mean any disrespect."

I pressed harder on Constantine's chest, fear filling me. "Let's go inside. I want to go inside now."

His stormy gaze sliced to me, then he hooked me around the waist, lifted me, and with my feet dangling above the ground, he carried me back across the garden to the house.

"Why are you angry?" I asked as he strode into the house. I'd caused this. I just wasn't sure how? "Constantine? Please?"

He stopped suddenly and placed me on my feet, his hands gripping my shoulders. "No other male is ever permitted to touch you. Not under any circumstances. Especially not to dance. His hands were on your fucking waist, you were touching him." His face twisted. "You need to understand that I am not like any other male you know, Delphine."

I wanted to shrink back, but I forced myself to speak up. "Besides my stepfather and a couple of his friends, you are the only male I've ever been permitted to speak to. Even before you found me at sixteen, I was sheltered and restricted."

His nostrils flared, and he muttered a curse word under his breath, some of his anger subsiding.

"I'm just trying to make friends," I said, willing him to understand.

"John's staff, he's not your friend. If you want friends, I'll make sure you get more time with my brothers' females. You're not to be friends with any males, Delphine, do you understand? And you're definitely not permitted to dance with them."

I nodded. "Okay," I said. "I just...I really liked the music, and I wanted to move to it. I was never allowed to listen to music like that, and the first time I ever really danced was with you."

His hands slipped down to my waist, and they flexed, digging in. "You weren't allowed to dance?"

"Douglas said it wasn't what well-bred females did."

His mouth hardened. "Douglas is a fucking asshole."

After their confrontation at the ceremony, his words didn't surprise me. "You really don't like him, do you?"

He held my gaze as if he were searching for something. "Do you?"

I licked my lips, my belly gripping uneasily. "Of course, I do," I lied.

"You can tell me the truth, Delphine. Remember, that's what bonded couples do."

I'd been taught how wrong it was to speak ill of your parents. Douglas had made it clear that disloyalty to family was the worst crime a person could commit. He wasn't here, though, he couldn't hear me, but even the thought of saying it out loud, how I truly felt, sent fear arrowing through me, and I found myself saying the words he demanded of me whenever I angered him. "I love my stepfather. He took care of me when my own father left us. He provided for me and my mother nearly all my life. I'm incredibly grateful to him and all he did for us."

Constantine continued to study me for several seconds, his expression unreadable, then it softened slightly. "Go upstairs and put on a pretty dress."

"Why?"

He chuckled. I stilled, surprised and delighted. I'd never heard him make that sound before, it was dark and rough and made my belly curl. "You'll never just do what you're told, will you, my curious little bride?" He tucked my hair behind my ear. "I'm taking you dancing."

Constantine

The Bank was a popular club frequented by humans and *others*, and a front for a second club below it. The Vault was one of the few feeding clubs that catered to blood drinkers in Roxburgh.

Nero had opened the place about ten years ago, choosing to spend more time here in the city than at the border. Nero was also the oldest among us, and had more than served his time. He'd been fighting the fae long before the rest of us were even able to pick up a sword. Now he was the monster we sent in to do the job when everyone else had failed. He preferred to work alone, was utterly deadly, and if he still felt a sliver of emotion, he didn't show it.

I wondered how his bride was faring. Nero wasn't just made of ice, he had particular tastes, and young and innocent had never been his preference.

I sat back in my chair and scanned the club.

Tonight, instead of the place being packed with customers, the only beings dancing were our brides. I nursed my glass, watching as Delphine laughed with the other females, her cheeks flushed and eyes bright.

"Any more trouble from Albertan?" August asked.

I glanced at him. "He sent two more assassins this last week. I dealt with it." I made sure they never left.

"Does Delphine know?"

I shook my head. "I've increased security, especially the garden where she likes to spend time. She has no idea what's going on. It helps that my guards are good at concealing themselves."

"Put him down and be done with it," Nero said.

I planned to. Douglas was relentless, determined...desperate, and it was only a matter of time before he made a mistake because of it, but I couldn't just kill the male. "We're not on the battlefield anymore. I need proof for the court, and both assassins died before I could get anything out of them."

Stefan's silver rings glinted as he placed another bottle of whisky on the table. Nero slid it his way, filling his glass to the top. His usual icy exterior exuded something else, something dark and volatile, and his gaze had only briefly left his female since they'd arrived.

It was the most I'd ever felt from him. "Problem?" I asked.

"My mate is willful. She taunts me, does not fear me, and refuses to acknowledge my authority."

I glanced over at Nero's bride, Mina. She was standing opposite Delphine, and wearing what had obviously once been a pink dress. She'd cut off the sleeves and chopped it so it was short, just above mid-thigh. She glanced our way, and when she saw Nero watching her, she lifted her chin and turned her back on him.

He growled under his breath.

"And that just makes you want her more?" August asked, knowing our brother all too well.

Nero's always stoney expression cracked and he actually scowled. "Yes." He downed the entire glass and refilled it. "She says she won't have me."

Stefan chuckled. "That'd be a first, brother."

Females fell all over the cold male when he was in The Vault, all wanting him to feed from them, fuck them, except for his bonded, apparently.

"He's never had to work for it in his very long life. I'd say the fates knew what they were doing when they sent her," Rainer said. "Nothing worth having comes easily."

"Is that right? And have you mated your female yet?" I asked Rainer.

"I took Lucinda last night," he said, surprising the hell out of me.

"You did?" Rainer had been as against taking a mate as I was. "What changed your mind?"

"The beast made the decision for me," he said, his mouth twisting to the side.

"The beast?" My brother had an inner beast he'd been fighting his entire life. When it reared up, they were at odds, always.

"Yes."

"It didn't frighten her?" When it came to the fore, he completely transformed.

He took another sip of his drink and shook his head. "No, she...tamed it, Con. She fucking tamed the beast. And he's been quiet, content since, for the first time in my entire life." He turned to me. "I think...I think mating with Lucinda is the best thing I've ever done. Don't resist," he said to the four of us sitting around him. "The fates chose those females for us for a reason. Denying them, denying the bond between us, is denying the kind of happiness we've only ever dreamed of."

I didn't know what to say. I sure as fuck didn't want to hear it. I tightened my fist around my glass. "You know why I can't mate Delphine. You fucking know."

"Samara wasn't your mate, Con," Rainer said. "She didn't deserve the end she got, and Douglas Albertan deserves to die in agony for what he did. You were friends, and that's how you loved her and she you. There were no tearful goodbyes when you left for months on end. She was free to fuck who she liked and so were you. Don't throw away your chance at peace, at happiness, in favor of revenge. And if anyone would want to see you happy, it was Samara."

He didn't understand. How could he?

"No, she wasn't my mate," I said to Rainer. "But she'd been there for me when I needed her, since I was old enough to pick up a sword, and she deserves better than to be replaced by the daughter of the male who brutally murdered her."

"And what about Delphine?" Rainer asked. "What does she deserve? Like all our females, the moment we sensed them, the moment we claimed them, they've suffered. They've been alone and sheltered for years. We're the reason they became prisoners in their own homes, but we're supposed to be their escape from it as well. Now is that time. What will you do if you don't mate her? Go back to the border? Abandon her when she needs you most?"

His words struck a direct hit right through my sternum. "It's for the best," I said, even as everything in me roared against it.

"And you're okay with her being alone in that big house. Seeking out others to feed from, to find her pleasure with, because her mate refuses to meet her needs? Refuses to give her what was promised the day you found her and staked your claim?" he said.

Every word was like another slice to the unbeating muscle in my chest, twisting more and more. "I'm going to kill Douglas, the male Delphine loves like a father, you think she'll forgive me for that? It's the way it has to be. I'm done with this conversation." I'd never leave her without blood, I was still letting, storing blood for her to feed on when I was gone. As for the rest, I couldn't bear to fucking think about it.

"Not hearing the truth won't change it," Rainer said.

Delphine's laughter drew my gaze back to her. Joy flowed from her, reaching out to me, wrapping around me so tight I suddenly had trouble drawing breath.

Rainer was right. She was owed that joy.

But I wasn't sure I could ever be the male to give it to her.

Ten

DELPHINE

Constantine held my hand as he led me from the club. I spun back and waved to my friends, and they waved back. I grinned, so incredibly happy.

We walked out onto the pavement. Morgan opened the car door and I got in, sliding across the seat. Constantine climbed in after me, and I threw my arms around him as soon as he pulled the door closed. I couldn't stop myself. "Thank you so much. I never knew it was possible to be this happy, and it's all because of you." I pressed a kiss to his cheek.

"I'm glad you had fun," he said.

"Fun? This was the best day of my life."

He did that thing he often did, where he went impossibly still.

"What is it?" I asked.

"Nothing."

I tightened my arms around his neck and kissed his cheek again, then leaned around and planted one on his lips, unable to hold back my joy. Laughter bubbled up inside me, and I didn't even try to hold it in. When I kissed him again, his hand shot up and gripped the back of my head, stopping me from pulling back.

Then he opened his mouth over mine and kissed me back. But

it wasn't like the little pecks I'd been giving him, it was one of his deep kisses that made me breathless and my body heat, with tongues and fangs and blood.

I climbed onto his lap and pressed closer. I couldn't seem to get close enough to him. One of his hands stayed in my hair while the other dropped to my bottom, to tug me tighter to him, as if he felt the same way, that close wasn't close enough.

We stayed like that, kissing, while I restlessly rocked against the hardness in his pants. When the car finally stopped, he shoved the door open and carried me inside, taking the stairs up to his room.

He set me on the bed, kneeling in front of me. His hands slid up under the skirt of my dress, then he gripped the sides of my underwear, tugging them down my legs and tossing them aside. "Hold your skirt up and spread your legs for me, Delphine. Show me how wet you got rubbing that pussy on me all the way here."

I did, eagerly, and he cursed. "Am I wet enough?"

He licked his lips. "You're perfect."

He rubbed his thumb along the seam of my folds and pressed in, making me gasp. One moment he was looking at me, the next his mouth was between my legs, his fingers sliding deep inside me. I fell back on the bed with a groan. Constantine was relentless, bringing me to a screaming orgasm in moments, then again, and again. His fingers inside me, while he licked and sucked until I was trembling, sweaty and smeared with blood from his delicious bites.

"Once more," he said.

I groaned and shoved at his head, then with the first lick, I yanked him back. I couldn't get enough of him, of this feeling he gave me. I came again, crying out his name and collapsed back in a boneless heap.

I lay there unmoving, sensing Constantine stand over me before he lifted me, shifting me up the bed, then tucked the covers around me. I passed out moments later.

~

I woke to the sound of running water.

Constantine's room was dark, and I was in bed alone. I didn't know how long I'd been asleep, maybe an hour or so. But my body ached, in a good way. The things he'd done to me... I shivered. I loved the way he touched me, never imagined the kinds of pleasure he was able to give me.

A low groan came from the bathroom.

I bolted upright.

It came again, deeper this time.

I shoved back the covers, pulled on Constantine's discarded shirt, and rushed to the bathroom door. I'd never heard him make that noise before. Was he injured? The thought sent a wave of fear through me, and before I could think better of it, I pushed the bathroom door open.

I froze at the threshold.

Constantine stood in the shower. I'd never seen him naked before. I'd seen his bare chest, had explored it, but I'd never seen him like...this.

Through the glass, I could see the way every muscle rippled under his smooth, tan skin. He had warrior tattoos on his back and chest, his arms and hands, a couple on his thighs as well. One of his hands was against the glass wall, veins bulging in his forearm, his biceps bunched tight. His back was to me, and his well-muscled buttocks were clenched, his long, strong legs braced apart.

His head was dipped, and he was standing in an odd way. His other arm was moving. He groaned again, and concern had my feet moving me forward. I rounded the shower. He still hadn't seen me, his eyes closed, so focused on whatever it was he was doing. Then I was standing in front of him.

His hand was wrapped around the part of him I'd felt under me whenever we kissed, the part that grew hard. It was long and thick, and he had his fingers wrapped around it, sliding it up and back brutally.

His head shot up, his violet eyes snapping open and clashing with mine. His fangs were extended, his forehead broader, his cheekbones and chin sharp blades. I'd never seen him like this before. He looked so different. I stumbled back a step, my hand flying to my mouth.

He didn't stop what he was doing, he straightened, something in his wild eyes shifting, his lids heavy, lips peeled back. My gaze slid over him again, all of him, and a pulse began a steady urgent beat between my thighs. Pleasure, that's what I was seeing on his face. Raw and undiluted.

The kind of pleasure he gave me, he was giving himself now. He was touching himself, the way he'd encouraged me to touch myself, to make myself feel good. His gaze didn't waver from me, and I took a step closer, helplessly drawn back to him. There was a look in his eyes, as if he were pleading with me for something I didn't understand.

I closed the space between us, only a glass wall separating us now. His hand slid down the glass, palm wide, fingers long. He pressed his forehead to it with a snarl, and I dipped my gaze to what he was doing between his thighs. His hand moved faster, and that part of him seemed to grow thicker, longer.

I stepped closer still, and something came over me. I felt empty, the pulse deep inside growing more insistent, my thighs now slick from my own need. I let his shirt fall open, then lifted my hand, pressing it against his through the glass. My other hand went to my breast, and I squeezed my nipple the way Constantine had.

He was snarling, his gaze locked on what I was doing.

I licked my lips and slid my hand down my body, over my belly.

"Yes," he growled.

I wasn't sure what was happening, not entirely, but I wanted to do it. I wanted to feel good, and I wanted Constantine to feel good as well. I rubbed the sensitive nub that made my legs go weak, and sparks of pleasure shot through my body. I was already sensitive from Constantine's mouth and was at the brink within minutes. I leaned in, needing the wall for support, my forehead against the glass as well. His mouth was so close but completely out of reach.

"Now, Delphine," he growled.

I knew what he wanted. Somehow, I knew, and I came for him, unable to do anything but obey his command, crying out, barely holding myself upright. He roared, the sound echoing in the smaller space, and pumped his hand faster as a creamy fluid spurted from him onto the tiled floor and washed down the drain.

I panted as we stared at each other through the glass.

Then, finally, he straightened, turned off the shower and opened the door. He quickly ran a towel over himself, then scooped me into his arms and carried me back to bed.

"Constantine?"

"Shhh," he said.

"But—"

"No questions. Sleep."

I wanted to argue, but the tone of his voice, though gentle, brooked no argument. He got into bed beside me, and this time he didn't bother with pants, like he did every other time I was with him, and pulled me close against his body. His warmth soaked through me, and I was instantly drowsy.

I wanted to ask him why he'd never shared that with me before, why he was hiding it from me while he thought I slept. I opened my mouth to do just that.

"Sleep, Delphine," he said before I could get a word out.

So I did as he said. I snuggled back into him and closed my eyes.

The next time I woke, morning sun was peeping in below the curtains. Constantine was still beside me. He'd rolled to his back, and my front was plastered to his side. His thick, black lashes rested on his cheeks, and he lay still and silent. The covers sat low on his hips, and I carefully lifted to my elbow and studied his muscled and tattooed chest, his stomach and arms.

His skin was so smooth in some places, while other parts were rough with battle scars. I couldn't imagine the life he'd led, the places he'd been, and the danger he'd lived through. While I'd been locked away, Constantine had been fighting battles, and sneaking into enemy territory to defeat those who conspired to eliminate our kind.

He'd lived.

Really lived.

Something I could only imagine, and even then, what I imagined was limited by what I'd been permitted to see and hear. I took in his chest, then lower, over his stomach. It was rigid with tight muscle, and I couldn't resist reaching out and running a finger over the corrugated flesh. It tightened more. I looked up at him, but he was still asleep. I dropped my gaze farther, to the bulge under the sheet.

I'd seen it last night, that part of him, but not a close look, and my curiosity got the better of me. I glanced up at him again and carefully, slowly, lifted the sheet.

It lay across his stomach, thick and long. It was darker at the end, and thick veins ran along the length of it. I reached out and touched it, sliding my finger along the soft skin. It was hot and smooth, velvety, and so incredibly hard. I remembered how Constantine had held it, his fingers curled around it, stroking from the base to the tip.

Touching himself that way had driven him wild, the pleasure on his face unmistakable. He'd given me pleasure like that over and over again. I wanted to do that for him. I wanted to give him that in return.

I shifted closer and curled my fingers around him now, my hold gentle, and eased my hand up and back, then again. It grew even harder, longer in my hand with every stroke.

A hiss exploded from him, and my gaze shot to his face.

He was looking down his body, watching me, eyes blazing.

"Am I hurting you? Is this wrong?" I asked, desperate to do this right, to make him feel good. To please him.

His hand curled around my wrist, applying pressure. He was going to pull my hand away, to tell me to stop. "Delphine—"

"You looked so handsome lying there and I...I couldn't stop myself from...from touching you." I ran my fingers along his length again. "Please, don't tell me to stop. Let me make you feel good. Please."

The muscle in the side of his jaw jumped. "Spit on it."

"What?"

He cupped the back of my head, pushing me closer to the hard length of him. "Spit, Delphine."

It seemed a strange thing to do, but I did as he said. His hand, the one that was wrapped around my wrist, slid up to cover mine, and he guided me, moving my hand over his hard, silky length, my spit now easing the way.

Color slashed his cheeks and he groaned. "That's it. Don't stop."

"Does it feel good?" I asked, though I thought I knew the answer.

"Yes." He spread his legs wider. "Grip me tighter, sweetheart."

Sweetheart.

I ate up the sight of him, how he looked as I curled my fingers tighter around him. He made a hissing sound. He was made so differently to me. This part of him was big, so I used my other hand as well, and I couldn't take my eyes off him, from the way he reacted. His muscled body flexed and tightened. His stomach looked as if it were carved from stone, and his chest strained.

Clear liquid pooled at the tip, and I quickly looked up at him. "Should it do that?"

"Yes," he said through gritted teeth.

My hand was no longer gliding easily, I needed more spit, but my mouth was dry from just the sight of him, so handsome and strong, and god, out of control. So I let my fangs slide down, and sunk them into my palm, using my blood instead.

It slicked his skin, painting his length red.

"Fuck," Constantine groaned. "Faster."

I did, watching the hard flesh between my hands as I stroked him even faster.

"I'm close," he growled.

I wanted to ask to what, but the wild, taut expression on his face stole the words from my lips. I thought I knew what would happen, the same thing as in the shower. He was going to orgasm. That was something we could both do despite our physical differences.

Watching him this way had made me impossibly wet, and the empty feeling inside me grew more insistent. I thought about the way I was made, then studied the way Constantine was made. It was almost as if—as if we were made to fit together.

He groaned, his thighs flexing, his bottom lifting, and a snarl burst from his lips as that same creamy liquid I'd seen come from him in the shower spurted from the tip again.

It landed on his stomach, and I couldn't take my eyes off it. He liked the taste of me, would I like the taste of him? Some of the rigidness left the appendage in my hands, but it didn't soften completely. I reached out and slid my finger though the creamy liquid on his stomach. "What's this called?"

"Come."

"And this?" I squeezed his length again and he groaned.

"My cock."

I slid my finger through his come again, then lifted it and licked it from the tip of my finger. It was unusual, but not unpleasant. "Hmm...I think I like it."

"Jesus," Constantine said, and his cock pulsed in my hand.

"What?" I looked up while I sucked the last of it from my finger. "Am I not supposed to do that?"

He dragged in a deep breath and released it. "You can do whatever you like to me, nothing is wrong, remember?"

I studied him again. "I was thinking, the way we're made, it's like...it's like we're made to fit together," I said, telling him what I'd been thinking when I stroked him.

He said nothing for the longest time, then he hooked me under the arms and pulled me up his body, his hand sliding between my thighs, instantly making me moan. "Enough talking now, my wanton little bride."

I instantly forgot what we were talking about when he slid two thick fingers inside me, and his mouth took mine.

Eleven

CONSTANTINE

I stood from my desk after going over maps and treaties, new and old threats to us from those beyond our territory sent to me by the Vampire Court, and strode to the window, drawn there as if compelled. I may not be out in the field at the moment, but our warriors were kept busy. There was always something for me to oversee. Stefan and Rainer would be arriving soon to discuss strategy. The war was over, but we needed to remain vigilant.

All thoughts of battle slipped from my mind, though, when my gaze found Delphine.

Like she did most days, she was strolling among the roses. Today she had a basket filled with them. To put in my room, no doubt, and my office and the dining room. My house, usually quiet and dark and cold, had been filled with them nearly every day, their color and perfume leaving Delphine's mark all over the house.

I scanned the surrounding area. I knew she was safe, my guards were watching, patrolling the perimeter, but Douglas was still sending hired killers after me. I'd caught, tortured, and dispatched another one only a couple nights ago. He'd told me nothing, not because he refused, but because he didn't know anything. My fingers curled into a tight fist.

Delphine bent over, inspecting a rose, and as she breathed in the scent, I saw that same rapturous expression on her face that I'd seen the first time I laid eyes on her, when she was just sixteen years old in her parents' garden.

The tension seeped from my shoulders. She was utterly breathtaking then, in a sweet and vulnerable way, but even more so now. Now she was a grown female with the curves to match. The way she held herself, the way she moved, all of it drew me. Delphine held me captive, entranced.

I was in trouble.

My sweet, little bride had burrowed deep, and I wasn't sure I could resist making her mine.

The way we're made, it's like…it's like we're made to fit together.

I shoved my fingers through my hair and paced to the other side of my office. Her innocence, her trust in me with every part of her, the things she said, her curiosity, all of it was chipping away at me piece by piece.

She'd called me handsome, for fuck's sake. No one had ever called me that. I wasn't. I was brutish and scarred and ugly. What did Delphine see that no one else did?

Christ, I was undeserving of her attention, and every day that passed, she shattered another piece of my resolve, my unraveling emotions growing more acute. But no matter how badly I craved her, I couldn't have my Delphine. I couldn't keep her.

Samara deserved retribution for what Albertan did, and she would get it. I hadn't been able to give her everything she wanted from me; I'd left when she'd asked me not to, choosing war and death over her time and again. I'd driven her to seek refuge in that sadistic fucker's dungeon.

Samara was dead because of me. I couldn't let myself forget that. I didn't deserve peace or happiness.

Douglas had gotten away with his crimes long enough.

And proof or not, I would find a way to end him. I wouldn't mate Delphine, tying her to me for life, when she'd only end up despising me for killing her stepfather, the male she loved like a father. Because no matter what, I would find a way. He would die at my hand.

Delphine

I'd spent most of the afternoon in the garden, enjoying the warm breeze. This morning had been too bright, but when the sun disappeared behind the clouds, and they'd grown heavy and gray, I'd rushed out.

Constantine had been in his office all morning, poring over maps and other papers. The more time he spent in there, the more concerned I became. John said he'd leave soon, that he'd return to the field, and the more time he spent in his office with those maps, the more I believed he might be right.

I hadn't been able to bring myself to just ask him, afraid he'd confirm it—afraid of what my reaction would be.

Two of his brothers were in there with him now. I'd heard their murmured voices, but I didn't know what they were talking about. Whatever it was, they sounded serious.

It was time to go back inside, it would soon be nightfall, but I wanted to enjoy the garden a little longer.

I took a moment to breathe in the scents coming from the different varieties of roses, then picked another of the lush red ones and put it in my basket, smiling as I brushed my fingers over their petals.

"I didn't think I'd see you today," John said, startling me. He was leaning against the trunk of one of the large oak trees, his hands in his pockets, eyes bright in the waning light.

"I had to wait until it grew cloudy to come out. The sun was a bit bright today."

"Ah, of course... I forget how young and innocent you are. How easily you could get hurt."

"Not so innocent," I said, not wanting him to think me naive. I hated that.

"Oh," he said with a chuckle. "Mr. Caputo's finally mated you, then?"

I wasn't sure I wanted to talk about that. It felt too private, something that had been bothering me, and something I wanted to keep between Constantine and me.

John's head tilted to the side. "No? Has he at least explained what you must do?"

"Of course," I lied, not wanting to admit the truth for some reason.

He nodded and glanced toward the house. "I'm glad to hear it. Where is he? Why isn't he with you now?"

"He's with his brothers."

"I expect they'll be discussing his return to the field? They're probably preparing for his departure."

My fingers curled tighter around the handle of my basket. "No, he wouldn't do that."

"I'm sorry, but he's a warrior, Del, it's what they do." A look of pity covered his face. "I'm surprised he'd do that with you unmated, though. He'd be leaving you vulnerable."

The feeling that shifted through me wasn't one I liked; no I hated it. Would he really do that? He'd declared his intention to claim me when I was sixteen, he'd come to the blood moon ceremony, we were blood bonded. Why wouldn't he take the final step and mate with me? What was wrong with me? "He wouldn't do that." Would he? Constantine was so closed off. I never knew what he was thinking or feeling. What if he did? What if he left me here vulnerable.

My stepfather could come for me—

"If he truly wanted to, Del, he would have mated you already."

I stumbled back a step.

"I'm not trying to hurt you. But honestly, I can't think of a reason for him to put your mating off. I'm your friend, remember? Friends tell each other the things that they need to know, even if it hurts." He closed the space between us. "Look, I wanted to tell you I'm leaving."

"Leaving? Why?"

"My family needs me, my father's sick," he said and leaned in. "I hate to leave when you're so upset...look, I know this sounds crazy, but I care about you, the time we've spent together in this garden the last few weeks has meant so much to me; you mean so much to me, and I don't like seeing you hurt like this...see Constantine hurt you like this, so if you ever want to get away from here, call me and I'll help you. I can keep you safe. I have money saved, I can get you far enough away that he'll never find you." He pulled a piece of paper from his pocket and handed it to me. "My number."

I opened my mouth to tell him no, to tell him what he said wasn't true, but the doubts I'd been fighting rushed to the surface. What if that was the truth of it? That Constantine didn't want me and would never mate with me."

"Just think about it," he said. "Something's not right with this whole situation. You have to see that."

I took another step back. "I need to go inside now."

"I'm sorry, Delphine. I really am, but living in some fantasy world will only hurt you more in the long run."

I nodded and spun around.

"You know how to reach me if you change your mind," he called after me.

I ran across the gardens and into the house.

Constantine and his brothers were still in his office.

My mind spun and pain battered my heart. I didn't know what to think. I walked into the library and shut myself in. Besides Constantine's bedroom, this was my favorite place in the house.

And right then, I needed an escape.

I searched the shelves for something to read, something to get me out of my head. There was a small book buried among Alice's romance novels. It had a female on the cover and a male stood behind her, one of his hands on her breast, his mouth at her throat. *Taken by the Dark Prince* was scrawled on the front. I'd finished the last book Alice had given me. So far, they'd been sweet and funny. I'd enjoyed the hugging and kissing I'd read in them.

Now I remembered what Lucinda said about Rainer threatening to *take her*. Could this book give me the answers I needed? I hoped so because Constantine wouldn't tell me, and I was sick of being kept in the dark. I'd been lied to and sheltered my entire life. Well, I was done with that. Those thoughts were all twisted up with the things John said and what it all meant.

I sat in one of the chairs and opened the book.

An hour later, it was dark outside, and I sat back in my chair, mind spinning. I'd been right.

Our bodies *were* meant to fit together. That's how the couple in the book had mated. I'd had to flip through several chapters to find it, but I had. Why didn't Constantine want to do that with me? Why did he keep avoiding my questions? When I'd asked him about it, he'd not answered me. I realized now he'd distracted me with pleasure.

I heard voices in the hall, the front door opening and closing, then Constantine going back into his office and shutting himself inside. I got up, slipped out of the library, then rushed up the stairs to my room. I showered quickly and fixed my hair, then put on my underwear and nightgown before slipping on my robe.

That's what the female in the book had done. She'd made herself look appealing so she could "seduce" her male. John said Constantine didn't want me. If that were true, then this wouldn't work.

When he walked into the blood moon ceremony, when he took my hand and led me from the room, he was telling everyone, just by being there, that he planned to make me his mate. I had to believe that. I had to believe he wanted it. Still, the idea that he'd changed his mind, that he didn't want me as his mate anymore, that I might be facing a future alone and unwanted—without Constantine...

I wrapped my arms around myself.

No. John was wrong. He had to be.

I shoved those thoughts from my mind and rushed down the stairs. Calling on every ounce of courage I possessed.

His office door was still closed, so I knocked lightly.

"Come in, Delphine."

He always knew when it was me. I bit my lip and opened the door with a smile and my hand planted on my hip, the same way the female in my book had. He didn't look up, busy reading something. He was frowning.

I thought about the scene I'd read and straightened my spine, moving to stand in front of his desk...then dropped my robe. "Constantine?"

"Mmm." He glanced up and froze.

I smiled brightly.

He sat back. "What are you doing?"

I walked around the desk. "Trying to seduce you."

His brows shot up. "How do you even know what that means?"

"A book I found in the library."

His eyes narrowed. "What book?"

"*Taken by the Dark Prince*."

"That's not one of my books," he said.

"No, it's Alice's. She's given me several books to read, but they only had kissing, this one had *taking* as well."

"Taking?"

"Yes, they also called it fucking in the novel, and I want you to do that with me, please."

His eyes closed and he drew in a breath, then let it out harshly. "Get me the book."

"Constantine—"

"Now."

I jumped at the demand in his voice, the quiet, contained fury, and snatched my robe from the floor, yanked it back on, and rushed off to do as he bid, my heart hammering in my chest. I grabbed the book and ran back.

He hadn't moved, just held out his hand.

I gave it to him.

"What page?"

I took it back and flipped to where it started and handed it back. I watched as he read it, his jaw tight, the veins in his forearm bulging as he gripped the novel, and the look on his face that—oh god—I wanted to shrink, to disappear. Disgust, that's what I saw. John was right, Constantine didn't want to mate with me. I was desperate for him, and he was repulsed at the very idea. What had I done wrong? Why had he changed his mind?

He was going to leave me.

I shook as tears welled in my eyes, until they couldn't be contained any longer and spilled onto my cheeks. This hurt. So much. More than anything had in my entire life. My throat burned from swallowing down my sobs. As he lowered the book, I dropped my head, letting my hair fall forward, covering my tear-soaked face, utterly humiliated.

"Come here."

Even after seeing that look on his face, his low demand had

embers of lust bursting into flame. I did as he said, because what else could I do? I had become the property of my stepfather when he mated my mother, and now I belonged to Constantine. It didn't matter that he didn't want me the way a male should want his mate.

"Look at me," he growled.

I shook my head.

"Now."

His tone sent a shiver through me, and I wasn't sure if it was born from fear or desire, maybe a little of both. I lifted my head, and Constantine flinched.

"Why are you crying?"

How could he not know how much he was hurting me? How could he be so blind? My own fury filled me, and for the first time in my life, I wasn't afraid to let it free. Whatever the consequences, I was prepared to pay them. For once, I would not bite my tongue. I would not smile and pretend I was okay with whatever meager crumbs of kindness someone gave me, or that my heart was surrounded by iron armor and their cruelty didn't cause damage with every disdainful look or harsh word.

"Why did you even claim me?" I cried, for the first time, since I was a child, raising my voice in anger. "Why did you come to the blood moon ceremony?" He reached for me, and I stepped back. "No. No, you don't touch me, not anymore. I thought you were my escape from Hell, but you only brought me to a new one. And this one is so much worse, because you gave me hope, over and over again, then each time you snatched it away. You say nice things or give me pleasure, then you hold me at a distance like I'm an inconvenience or an annoyance. I offer myself to you, and you sit there and cut me to pieces with your look of disgust."

He stood, his shock at my outburst written all over his face. "Sweetheart—"

"I'm not your sweetheart, and I don't want to be here anymore. Release me. Let me go, because this hurts too much."

His mouth twisted, his eyes growing wild. He took a step toward me, his face thrown in shadow, concealing his features.

"No," I said again and backed up several more steps. "I don't want you to touch me."

His chest expanded, and when he took another step closer, light from the lamp bathed the side of his face. I gasped. He was transformed, like he had in the shower, but even more so, his face all sharp angles, his fangs long and vicious, his eyes glowing and vibrant. I was looking into the eyes of a monster.

I fell back another step.

"Do not run, Delphine," he snarled. "Whatever you do, do not run from me."

Twelve

CONSTANTINE

Delphine took another step back.

"Don't you fucking run," I snarled again. The monster had roared to the surface as soon as I'd seen her tears. Then she'd gone and laid out all the ways I'd hurt her, that she wanted to leave me, and the predator was ready to do anything to stop that. If my heart could beat, it would be pounding in my chest, as it was, adrenaline coursed through me so hard and fast my head spun.

Delphine stared at me, bloody tears glistening on her cheeks, shaking with her anger and hurt.

"Delphine," I growled.

Her shoulders stiffened.

"Don't—"

She spun around and ran from the room.

I snapped. Anger, fear, excitement flooded my system. There was no stopping the predator now. She glanced over her shoulder, her robe flowing out behind her as she tore down the hall, her eyes widening when she saw me coming. She ran into the library and slammed the door after her, locking it. I kicked it open, fully in the monster's control now, and there was nothing and no one that would stop me from getting to my female, not even her.

The doors leading out to the garden were wide, the curtains billowing from the warm summer breeze. "Delphine," I roared, going after her. Moonlight lit up the garden. She was running between two rose beds, the silk of her robe catching the light.

I had her.

My little bride was fast, but she had no idea how fast I was. My adrenaline spiked again, anticipation rolling through me like thunder, quaking me to my core as I pounded after her, closing the gap fast.

She glanced over her shoulder again and cried out a moment before I pounced, taking her down and using my body to shield hers from the impact. As soon as I hit the ground, I flipped her to her back and pinned her to the grass beneath us.

She looked up at me, panting.

"I told you not to run, Delphine...now look what you've made me do."

"Get off me," she shrieked and shoved at me.

I leaned in, dragging my nose up the side of her throat, breathing in the scent of her skin, sinking deeper under her thrall.

"Why did you come after me? You don't want me. Let me go. I don't want to be here anymore. I don't want you either." More tears streamed down her face.

Her tears told me that she felt the complete opposite, as did her scent. "You're wet, little one. You want me right here. Right where I am."

Her face darkened. "Why are you doing this to me? Do you truly hate me this much? What did I ever do to you, Constantine? What did I do?"

"Hate you? I don't hate you." What I felt was the complete opposite despite all my efforts to stop it from happening.

Her chest rose and fell against mine. "You don't want me."

With a snarl, I shoved her legs wide and ground my hard cock against her, making her gasp. "You feel that? That's how hard you make me, that's how much I want you. I haven't stopped wanting you since I saw you up at that window looking down at me."

Her wide gaze searched mine. "Then...then why won't you make me yours in truth?" she said, her lip trembling.

Right then, I couldn't think of an answer. Not with the monster in control, with my head spinning and my body roaring for her, to take her like she wanted me to. Like I'd wanted to since the moment I'd laid eyes on her.

I shoved my hand between us, pulled up her nightgown, and slid my fingers down the front of her pretty underwear. She was hot and so fucking slick. Her whimper turned my gut inside out and set my blood on fire. I pushed two fingers in deep, and she cried out. Staring into her eyes, I fucked her with my fingers, staying deep, concentrating on the spot inside her that would get her off hard and fast. She fisted my hair with one hand and dug her nails into my shoulder with the other, shoving me away, then pulling me back. Shaking her head to deny me, then begging me for more.

She tried to turn away, and I grabbed her jaw and made her look at me as I quickly and roughly brought her to orgasm. Her luscious mouth dropped open, and she cried out, coming hard around my fingers.

"You are mine, Delphine. I won't ever let you leave, understand?"

"No, I don't. I don't understand." She shook her head. "Tell me, tell me what you want from me, because I don't understand any of this."

Her plea smashed into me, and I knew I was about to throw all my plans out the window for my little bride. She was hurting because of me. I'd been careless with her feelings, the same way I had been with Samara. The thought of losing Delphine as well. No, I couldn't bear to even think about it, not now.

I couldn't fight this anymore. I should, but my need for her, to keep her, to protect her, was far too strong.

I'd have to figure out another way to destroy Douglas, but it couldn't be at the expense of Delphine's happiness, and yes, my own. It was extremely difficult, but I gentled my grip on her. "I know you don't, so I'm going to show you." I used my fangs to bite into my palm, allowing blood to pool in my cupped hand, then brought it down and smeared it over her pussy.

"What are you doing?"

I should take her inside, to my bed, but now that I'd made up my mind, I couldn't wait even a second longer than I had to. "I'm making you as wet as I can, because I'm a big male and you're small, especially here," I said and slid my finger inside her again, slicking her with more of my blood. "And when I take you, I want to make it as painless as I can."

She jerked beneath me. "Take me?"

I pressed my forehead against hers as I tore her panties from her body. "I tried to resist because I thought that was the best thing for you. I see now I was wrong, Delphine, and I'm done resisting. You are mine." I tore my shirt off, throwing it aside, and quickly undid my pants, freeing my cock. "I'm going to make you mine for eternity."

She trembled. "You really want me?"

"More than anyone or anything." I took her mouth in a hard kiss as I pressed the head of my cock to her tight opening. "It might hurt, but not for long, and only this once, okay?"

"Okay," she said and licked her lips.

"Kiss me," I rasped.

She did, and slicking my length with more of my blood, I applied more pressure, pushing in a little. Delphine groaned, her arms banding around me. She only had the tip. Fuck, so tight. I pushed in another inch.

She whimpered. "It's too much," she said and dug her nails into my back.

I held her gaze as I pushed in another inch. "You can take me, because you were made for me. You need to relax. Relax and let me in." My mind spun, and her tight grip had me gritting my teeth.

She whimpered again and moaned my name. "It's too big."

Panic filled me because hurting her wasn't something I could tolerate. "It's okay, sweetheart," I said, pressing kisses to her parted lips. "It's going to be okay. Relax for me, let me in."

"I don't think I can," she cried.

Another tear streaked down her cheek, and I kissed it away. "It'll be good, I promise. You just have to relax."

"I don't know how."

She was stiff, every muscle locked tight. I bit into my palm again, coating her with more of my blood as I tried to ease in some more. She cried out, but not in pleasure, and it was as if she'd plunged a dagger into my chest.

She squeezed her eyes shut, panting and squirming under me.

"Look at me, Delphine," I said, though it came out more of an unhinged growl.

She blinked up at me and more tears streaked down her cheeks.

Christ, she was ripping me to shreds even as the urge to thrust deep, to claim her, to take her, was close to sending me insane. "You trust me to make you feel good, don't you, little one?"

"Y-yes."

My hand was still between us, and I circled her clit with my blood-covered fingers. She gasped. "Focus on what my fingers are doing, not my cock, okay? Focus on how good that feels."

She nodded, and as I circled her clit again, then brushed over it, I felt her relax a little around the head of my cock. "That's it. Feels good?" All color had drained from her face when I started pushing inside her, pink hit her cheeks again now.

She licked her lips. "Yes, don't stop."

I kissed her. "That's good, that's my good girl."

Her nails eased up and her thighs that had been locked to my sides relaxed some as well. I worked her clit faster, biting back my growl so I didn't scare her when I felt her muscles relax even more. She was panting now.

I eased the tip of my cock out a little, then back in and she groaned, and the sound was pure pleasure. I did it again, and this time when I slid back in, I took another inch.

"Constantine," she said, her voice a little panicked, but not from fear.

Her thighs trembled, and I pressed down on top of her, holding my forehead to hers. "This might pinch," I said and slid all the way in, stuffing my female with every hard inch of me.

She arched against me helplessly and screamed out in shock. "It hurts." She shoved at me.

I grabbed her flailing hands in one of mine and lifted them over her head. "Hold still," I whispered roughly as I did the same, all except for my thumb at her clit.

Her breaths puffed out, hard and fast, as I held utterly still. "Talk to me? Does it still hurt?" I could bite her now and send her over the edge, but I wanted her right here with me. I wanted her to remember every second of this moment, not lost in my bite, forced to feel good.

She looked down between us and I lifted my chest from hers so she could see. "A little, but not so much now. It feels strange." Her gaze was on my thumb working her clit, and she released a shuddery breath, her muscles squeezing around my cock. "I think...oh, I think I'm going to—" She threw her head back and cried out, spasming around me as she came.

I gritted my teeth as her pussy fucking milked my cock. I forced myself not to move until she quieted, until she stilled under me. As soon as she did, I tested her resistance and eased out halfway, then back in.

"Oh god," she said, her nails digging into my shoulders again, holding me closer.

I did it again, almost all the way out and back in, and we both moaned. "Good?"

"Y-yes…please," she said, and her hands slid down my back. "More."

That was all I needed to hear. I started fucking her then, nowhere near as hard and deep as I wanted to, but even still, nothing had felt as good as being buried inside Delphine. This was where I was supposed to be. This was pleasure and joy and happiness and fear all rolled into one.

Emotions I'd been steadily losing over the centuries were now right there on the surface. God, they were vibrant, a fucking wild storm inside me, because of the sweet little female clutching me to her so damn tight.

Now I was here, the idea of losing her, of losing this, wasn't something I could bear to contemplate.

This was home.

Delphine was home.

I kissed her as I took her, her hands moving over my back, my shoulders, her thighs wrapped tight around me, holding me to her. Why didn't anyone tell me? Why didn't anyone warn me? This was —it was all-consuming perfection.

"More, Constantine," she gasped.

I cupped her face with one hand and slid the other beneath her hips, lifting her higher as I thrust faster, harder inside her. "You're so beautiful, Delphine." I kissed her jaw, her throat. "All mine."

"Yes," she groaned.

My fangs tingled, and I didn't even try and resist. I bit into her silkin flesh, her blood filling my mouth. Delphine screamed, coming around me again, shaking and crying out.

I took one more pull, then sealed the bite before leading her mouth to my throat. "Bite," I growled out.

My little bride struck, instantly, pulling hard on my vein. There was no holding back after that, I slammed inside her and came with a roar, filling my mate over and over until we were done.

Until both of us were boneless, under the full moon, surrounded by roses.

And wrapped in each other's arms.

Thirteen

DELPHINE

CONSTANTINE'S ARMS banded around me, and he rolled so I was on top of his big body, his cock still deep inside me, my mouth attached to his throat.

I'd bitten him so many times, his chest was streaked with blood, and still I couldn't get enough. He strained beneath me, snarling and groaning as he held back his orgasm, when each of my bites took him right to the edge.

It spoke of his age and control, something I didn't have. As soon as Constantine bit me, I flew apart. But having him deep inside me got me there as well. I'd lost count of the number of times I'd come the last few days. We'd barely left his bed since he picked me up off the ground in the garden and carried me up to his room.

I rocked my hips, moving him inside me as I lapped at the bite, licked up the trail of blood, and struck again on the other side.

"Fuck, Delphine," Constantine gasped, his hips lifting.

I pressed down, taking him as deep as I could, something I'd learned felt wonderful, and then circled my hips. My moan was low and wanton. Constantine hooked me around the back of the neck and pulled me down, his eyes locking on mine. He liked looking into my eyes when I came. I shook, losing control.

As soon as my cry burst from me, he let go, his hand sliding down my back and gripping my hip, holding me down on him as he throbbed, pulsing inside me.

I fell against his chest, and he wrapped me in his arms. Exhaustion hit me hard and my eyes were already drifting shut.

He rubbed my back, his mouth going to my ear. "Rest, sweetheart."

I smiled. I loved when he called me that. I hugged him back tighter and let sleep claim me.

It was still dark when I woke. I had no idea what pulled me from my sleep, but Constantine wasn't beside me anymore. I sat up, a strange feeling in my belly.

Someone was downstairs, I heard voices.

I shoved back the covers, dragged on my robe, and rushed to the door, easing it open.

Morgan was talking fast to one of the other guards. Constantine was nowhere to be seen. Tying the sash on my robe, I ran down the stairs. Morgan straightened when he saw me, both males going quiet.

I held my robe closed at my throat. "What's going on?"

"Nothing for you to be concerned about, I assure you. I'm sorry we woke you," he said.

"Where's Constantine?"

The front door opened and my mate walked in. He was in only a pair of trousers and his chest was splattered with blood, not his, not from me, this was fresh.

I rushed toward him, and he lifted his hands, stopping me. "Go back to bed, Delphine. I'll be up soon."

"What happened? What's going on?"

He strode up to me and took my shoulders in his hands. "Please, for once, can you do as I ask without question or resistance?"

I shook my head. "Tell me what happened to you—"

He took my face in his hands, his eyes locking on mine. "Please, I need you to do as I ask."

He was serious, deadly. I wanted to keep questioning him, but the look in his eyes told me I needed to do as he said. I nodded and rushed back upstairs, my belly in knots.

Hours passed. I tried to stay awake, but despite my nerves and worry, the last few days and nights with Constantine made it impossible. I couldn't keep my eyes open.

The next time I woke it was early morning. I heard voices outside and quickly got out of bed and rushed to the window. Constantine and a female stood by his car, she had black hair and her head was dipped. They stood close, deep in conversation—

He pulled her into his arms, holding her tight. I froze, watching in horror as he ducked his head to see her face, pressed a kiss to the top of her head, then took her hand and led her to the passenger side. She got in, then he strode around the car and did the same.

I spun from the window and ran out of the bedroom and down the stairs.

Morgan was at the bottom, but this time he was on his own and it was obvious he was waiting for me. He got in my way when I tried to pass.

"You have to stay inside," he said.

"Where's Constantine going? Who was that with him?" I asked, trying to get around him.

Sympathy covered Morgan's face as he stood in my way again. "He wanted to tell you himself, but things happened fast last night—"

"Tell me what?" My heart pounded. "Where is he going, Morgan? Why was he with that female?"

"He had to leave."

"Leave? What are you talking about? He wouldn't just leave, not without telling me. He wouldn't. I don't understand."

Morgan's expression didn't change. "There's unrest with the fae, and he's needed. He didn't have time to tell you."

I saw him, right here. We spoke. He could have told me then. "How long will he be gone?"

"I'm not sure, I'm sorry. I wish I could tell you more."

"Who was she? The female, tell me, Morgan."

His gaze slid from me. "A warrior. She'll be accompanying him."

Why wouldn't he look me in the eyes? He was lying to me. "What about his brothers, are they going with him?"

He shook his head. "They weren't needed. He took Veera instead. They'll head to our territory's border and be back as soon as Constantine has everything under control."

What? Why wouldn't the others go with him? They were the fiercest warriors of our race. "I don't understand. None of this makes sense."

"I'm sorry, that's all I can tell you."

I tried to walk around him once more and he shook his head. "Constantine wants you to remain indoors for now."

I didn't understand any of this. Why didn't Constantine say goodbye? Why was he with that female? He was being soft with her, the way he was with me. He kissed her, he held her hand.

Morgan took a step closer. "I'm sorry. Delphine..."

I spun and ran back up the stairs and to the window.

The car was gone.

My mate was gone.

He'd left, and he hadn't even said goodbye.

I stood at the door to the library, staring out at the garden through the rain-streaked glass. My roses were the only bright thing in my world. Memories of what Constantine and I did out there filled my mind.

He'd been gone three weeks. He'd called to speak to me several times, but he seemed distracted and gave no indication of when he was coming home, and I wondered if he was ever going to. No one would tell me anything, and I was still confined indoors. I was close to losing my mind. I really needed a friend, more than ever, but John was gone. Even Alice was acting strange. I'd seen her watching me as closely as the other security. Whenever I got close to one of the doors, one of them appeared.

It was as if I were back with my parents, locked away, alone all the time. Lonely. I'd had a taste of happiness, of pleasure, of love, and freedom, and now it'd been snatched away from me with no explanation.

Whenever I closed my eyes I saw my mate with that female, with Veera, holding her hand, kissing the top of her head in a way that showed his affection for her. When I asked him about her the first time he called, he said the same as Morgan and ended the call.

But I could tell he was keeping something from me.

Nausea hit me at the thought of them together. I couldn't bear it.

Thunder rolled through the sky so close it seemed as if it were right above the house. I needed to talk to someone. I couldn't take much more.

I peeked out into the hall. Morgan was talking to Alice, deep in conversation. I zipped past while their backs were to me and into Constantine's office, quickly shutting myself in. He only ever used his cell phone, but there was an old landline phone in here as well. We'd had one in the kitchen at home that no one ever used.

I picked it up and quickly dialed the number I'd memorized.

The phone rang several times. "Hello?"

"John? Is that you?"

"Delphine...are you okay?"

My lips quivered before I even got a word out, my throat growing tight.

"Del?"

"Constantine's gone, and I'm trapped here, John. They say it's for my own good, but no one will tell me what's going on or why I have to stay inside."

There was a pause. "Constantine left without you?" His surprise was obvious and I felt humiliated all over again, that my mate could leave me so easily.

"He's gone to the fae border with Veera, one of his warriors."

There was another pause, then a sigh. "I'm so sorry, Del. I should have told you about her, but I didn't think she'd be an issue."

"What do you mean?"

"I really wish I wasn't the one to have to tell you this, but you know I tell you the truth because I care." He sighed again. "They're lovers, Del. Veera was at the house all the time before you arrived. I assumed he'd given her up, but I'd obviously been wrong."

I gripped the phone harder. "He wouldn't do that."

"He's a male, an old one. He's used to having whatever he wants. He won't go without a female in his bed."

I sat heavily in the chair behind the desk.

"You couldn't give him what he wanted," John added. "So he must have decided to go back to Veera. I can't help but wonder if she's the reason he put off mating you like he did. He was pining for her."

His words sliced my heart in two. I bit my lip, unable to bring myself to tell John I'd been stupid enough to mate with Constantine. He'd known what my life had been like, he'd made me believe he cared, then he left me anyway. Even the bond of mating wasn't strong enough to keep him here with me, to want only me. When I was so deeply in love with him, I was struggling to breathe from the pain of losing him.

"Veera wasn't his first love, though, that would be Samara. I don't think he ever recovered from her death."

It was as if he'd plunged a dagger into my chest. "What?"

"I think your stepfather knew her?"

"Douglas knew Constantine's…?" I didn't know what to call her.

"His love, yes. It's well known in certain circles that your stepfather took a liking to Samara and made her one of his playthings. This is all rumor, of course, no one could prove Mr. Albertan had anything to do with her disappearance. Constantine believed he did, though. But he hasn't been able to prove it, either, or he would've killed your stepfather a long time ago."

Constantine blamed Douglas for killing his first love? He'd never said anything about that to me.

"Maybe when he realized whose daughter you were, he changed his mind? Maybe the idea of mating with you disgusted him?"

Then I remembered my stepfather's reaction when he realized it was Constantine who would claim me.

Oh god.

John was telling the truth.

I knew what my stepfather was capable of. If Constantine thought Douglas had killed Samara, then he had. She was the reason Constantine and Douglas hated each other.

"Del, let me help you. I'll get you away from there."

"Constantine will come after me," I said.

There was a beat of silence. "Honestly, I'm not so sure he would. Not if claiming you was just some way to get back at your stepfather, and that's what it's starting to look like. I mean, Constantine made his grand entrance, took you from him, then never mated you, and now he's, for lack of a better word, stuck with you. I feel terrible I didn't share this with you sooner, but I didn't want to hurt you..."

I heard Alice call my name. I swallowed down my sob. "I have to go." I quickly hung up and slipped out of the office and rushed upstairs.

Alice was coming the other way, and her relief when she saw me was obvious. "I've been looking everywhere for you. Your meal's ready."

"I'm not hungry." John's words were on repeat in my head. I'd lost my appetite completely. Her look was disapproving, but I didn't care. "I'm going up to bed. Good night." It was early still, but sleep was the only escape from the pain and loneliness. I'd been sleeping a lot. Alice said I was depressed.

"You need to feed," she said as I walked by.

"I'll feed in the morning." Constantine had blood stored for me, a lot of it. He'd been letting when I first came here, but I assumed he'd stopped when I started feeding from him again. Apparently, he hadn't. John had been right, he was the only one who'd been truthful with me. Constantine hadn't wanted to make me his mate, and only had when I'd threatened to leave. That would've ruined his plan for revenge. He'd only mated with me to get back at Douglas. He'd always planned to leave, and he had months and months worth of blood stored for me for when that time came.

I kicked off my shoes, and climbed into Constantine's bed, my gaze immediately sliding to the rose on the bedside table, the one he'd left on my pillow. I'd carefully dried it, convinced it meant something deeper. That he felt something deeper for me. I curled my fingers into a tight fist. The urge to reach out and crush it, to stomp it into the carpet filled me, but I couldn't bring myself to do it.

I turned away. I'd brought it in here after he'd left, but I couldn't bear to look at it now. My heart was a lump in my chest. God, it hurt. I was in love with my mate, and he didn't care about me enough to even bid me farewell when he left on a trip with no end date in sight.

My stepfather had treated me like I was nothing, and now Constantine was doing the same.

The thought of him lying to me, of pretending to want me to hurt my stepfather was too painful to bear.

I'd let it happen. I'd allowed myself to be treated like property, like chattel—like nothing.

How long would I wait here, hoping that Constantine would come back to me, that he'd give me a few crumbs of affection, when that day might never come, and if he did come back, how long before I woke to discover him gone again? How much longer would I allow others to treat me this way?

The answer filled my head.

Not one more night.

Nerves filled me—fear—but I squashed it.

Not one more night.

I was leaving this place, and I wasn't coming back. Constantine didn't love me, and he never would. I refused to turn into my mother, cold and emotionless, and that's what would happen if I stayed here, if I allowed the pain to devour every emotion I had, until there was nothing left. I lay in bed, waiting for the house to quiet, for everyone to go to bed, then quickly packed only what I could carry.

I dressed in trousers and a sweater, pulling on a coat with a hood and a pair of sturdy boots, slung my bag over my shoulder, then slipped from the room. As I rushed quietly down the stairs, voices came from the library.

Morgan and another of the guards.

In the three weeks since Constantine had left, I'd never come down here at night, and I'd never attempted to leave. They wouldn't be expecting it now. I slipped past the library and into Constantine's office. A flash of lightning lit up the room momentarily, followed closely by thunder.

I rushed to the phone and dialed John's number for the second time that day.

"Delphine?"

"I'm so sorry to wake you."

"It's fine, I told you I'm here for you."

I looked around Constantine's office and my heart gripped in my chest. His scent was still so strong in here, it was like he'd walk through the door at any moment. But that wasn't going to happen. "I was wondering...if you could come and get me, please. I'd like to leave now."

There was a beat of silence. "Can you get to the back garden undetected? There's an old gate back there, behind the hedge. I can be there in twenty minutes. I'll wait for you on the other side."

"I'll be there." I disconnected, checked that the hall was clear, and headed toward the kitchen. That'd be the easiest way out, and the least likely chance of being seen.

I'd behaved, done everything I was told, and because of that, Morgan and the other security guards wouldn't expect me to try and leave now.

I made my way from the kitchen to the back garden without detection. I'd only had to hide once, behind one of the trees surrounding the grounds when a guard walked by.

John arrived a short time later, right where he said he'd be. He jumped out and rushed over to me. "Are you okay?"

I shook my head. "Please, get me away from here."

He pulled me in for a hug. "Anything you need, I'm here for you, Del. I promise I'll keep you safe."

I nodded even as the pain grew. The sooner I was away from here, the better. I would not spend one more moment in this loneliness. Not one more.

Fourteen

DELPHINE

My eyes opened when John's car drove over a pothole, then stopped suddenly.

A grogginess had come over me not long after we'd escaped in John's car. He'd stopped once for gas and got us a hot chocolate about fifteen minutes into our drive, to help calm me. I'd fallen asleep straight after and was having trouble opening my eyes now.

"John?"

"I'm here. You need to wake up now, sleepyhead."

I rubbed my eyes and blinked several times, feeling heavy and sluggish. My sight was blurred, and I blinked again when it cleared a little. I stared through the pelting rain. We were in front of a set of massive iron gates—gates that I recognized instantly, that I'd looked at from my bedroom window, wishing I could walk through them and never come back.

No.

I spun to John. "Why did you bring me here? We need to leave, quickly."

He stared at me, then smiled. It wasn't warm, and sent shards of ice down my spine. I grabbed for the door and tried to open it. But it was locked.

The gates opened.

"No, please. Take me away from here. Please." I grabbed his arm, but he shoved me off.

The front door opened and my stepfather walked out as we drove in.

Oh god.

I was going to die.

~

Constantine

I'd led them away from Delphine for three weeks. Taking them on a wild-goose chase while I picked them off one at a time. Douglas's assassins were relentless and skilled, but not more than me.

I'd managed to keep it from Delphine, but Douglas wanted me dead and his daughter back. I knew who he really was, and he was terrified I'd find a way to expose him. But mostly, he wanted the money and status he was promised, and Delphine was the best way for him to get both.

The attacks and attempted break-ins at my home had been increasing, but I'd had a handle on it, until the night before I left—four assassins had gotten onto the grounds, one of them into the fucking house. I'd killed three of them and tortured the fourth. He hadn't known who was paying for his services, everything had been kept anonymous, but there would be more coming, and they'd keep coming until I was dead.

I'd done the only thing I could, I'd led the danger away from my mate. I knew Delphine's stepfather was behind this, but until I had proof, she wasn't safe with me there.

I'd asked Veera, a warrior who had fought in the fae wars beside us, to play the role of Delphine and she'd agreed. She was similar enough that if she kept her head dipped, like my mate often had when she first came to me, they wouldn't know the difference. We'd put on a little show at the house before we left, to convince them it was Delphine, and I'd been right; they'd followed. There'd been no more attacks or attempted break-ins since we left.

My brothers, Morgan, the rest of my security, had taken turns watching over my home and Delphine after I left, in case things hadn't gone the way I suspected they would or if Douglas figured something was up and sent men back to the house.

Still, leaving Delphine had been the hardest thing I'd ever done. It was the only thing I could think of to keep her safe, though. I'd wanted to tell her why, but I wasn't sure how she'd react. Douglas was her family, like she'd said, he'd raised her, provided for her. She felt loyalty towards him, loved him like a father. If she knew the truth, she might try and leave me again. She might run and put herself in even more danger.

The end goal was her stepfather's death, at my hand. I didn't know yet how deep her loyalties or affection went where I was concerned, and I wasn't willing to test it yet and possibly lose her.

I knew my own feelings, though.

I would kill, maim, decimate anything or anyone that tried to harm her. My little mate had crawled so deep into my heart that I couldn't remember my life without her. I was in love with her. An emotion that had seemed an impossibility until Delphine moved into my home and waged war on the useless organ in my chest, chipping away at my defenses until they crumbled at her feet. Which was why I'd had to leave without telling her goodbye, and I'd kept our calls brief.

One word from her and I wouldn't have been able to leave her, one request for me to return and I'd be heading back to her in a heartbeat.

Veera held up two fingers and pointed to the shadows at the edge of the castle ruins.

I nodded. I'd seen them as well. We split up, and a short time later, both assassins were dead.

Veera wiped the blood from her chin. "They're relentless. These last few haven't been as skilled, but still, assassins don't come cheap."

They did not. "Someone has to be helping him. Douglas has money, but he's been careless with it over the years." Sure that whoever his daughter mated would top up his bank accounts, he hadn't seen the need to be careful. "Someone else has to be footing the bill."

"He's found another mate for your Delphine," she said.

That's exactly what he'd done. Anticipating my death, he'd sold her to the highest bidder. A female like Delphine would get a high price. Among males like Douglas there was a market for young, beautiful females, females from prominent families, widows with no mate or no protection, used as breeding stock for a much-needed heir, and of course, females like Samara, who they thought no one would miss.

Veera looked down at the dead vampires at our feet. "Douglas is getting desperate."

He was. But we finally had what we needed to force the court's hand and sign an execution order. Tomorrow we journeyed home.

My phone vibrated in my pocket, and I quickly checked it. Morgan. He was only to call in an emergency. "What is it? Is Delphine okay?"

There was a beat of silence. "She's gone, Constantine."

"What the fuck do you mean gone?"

"Some of her things are missing. And one of the guards saw John's car outside the grounds."

My mind roared, and the monster exploded to the surface. I was already running for the car, Veera right behind me. "I'm on my way." I jumped in the car, started it, and planted my foot on the gas. I'd fucked up. Delphine wouldn't leave me for another male, but I'd watched her grow in confidence. My brave little female would leave if she believed I'd abandoned her, and I could guarantee John had positioned himself to be the one to help her.

I had thorough background checks done on all my staff before I hired them. John's had been clean, but then some fuckers would do anything for money. It'd explain his sudden departure.

"You think this John works for Douglas?" Veera asked.

"Yes," I growled and almost tore the steering wheel off. There was no aging relative who needed his help, of that I was now certain. He left before I found out who he worked for. He was no assassin, there was no chance he could get the jump on me, but he could spy and report back, he could get in Delphine's ear and spread poison. I was going to find him and tear his throat out.

Douglas had Delphine, there was no doubt in my mind that's where John had taken my mate. Her stepfather might have a buyer for Delphine, but he'd take his pound of flesh from her first. He'd make her pay, even though she had no control over any of this, because he was a sadistic fuck.

He'd been careful with her up until the night of the blood moon ceremony because he'd had to be.

He didn't need to do that anymore.

Delphine was fair game, and that sick and twisted male was capable of anything.

Fifteen

DELPHINE

THE IRON MANACLES around my wrists dug in as I fought against them. "Please...don't." A scream burst from me as Douglas tore the white cotton dress from my back, exposing the deep cuts.

He'd used his whip on me earlier, and because I hadn't fed in several days, my wounds were slow to heal.

He grabbed a thick white bandage and wrapped it around my torso roughly. "You had one job, Delphine, to marry someone wealthy and influential. All you had to do was spread your fucking legs and mate with the right male. That's all. Instead you bond with a male who would leave us without our due."

A sob burst from me. "I—I had no control over who...m-my mate was." He knew that, logically he knew that. But he didn't seem to care about logic at all. His main focus since I arrived here two days ago had been to make me scream in pain, and I had, so much, my throat was raw.

He closed the distance between us. "It's only a matter of time before Constantine is dead. Thank fuck he didn't actually want you. Sir Bentham wouldn't take you if you'd been plowed by that monster of a male."

John had been reporting to my stepfather, telling him everything we'd talked about. He'd drugged me to get me here. I'd heard them talking before Douglas handed him money and he left.

My stepfather thought me still a virgin, that I hadn't mated, and I hadn't corrected him. The way he spoke of it, it was important to Sir Bentham. And I knew in my gut if I admitted I'd mated with Constantine, he'd be furious; that he'd end my life, but not before he'd tortured me far worse than he had already.

And even now, I couldn't help but hold out hope that Constantine would come for me. Despite everything, I believed he cared for me. Maybe not in the way he'd cared for Samara or Veera, but he'd been protective of me, territorial in the way of all older male vampires over their possessions.

Or maybe that was wishful thinking? My own mother hadn't come to my rescue, and she had to know I was down here. She knew everything that happened in this house. She just chose to turn a blind eye.

Douglas undid my manacles and pulled me down. "You need to look the part," he said and set my limp body in a chair, then pulled a blue ball gown over my head, dressing me like a doll. "You need to look good, and smile, or you'll pay for it afterward." He dragged a brush through my hair, dabbed blush on my pale cheeks, and smeared red lipstick across my lips.

He stood back. "There, that's better."

There was a knock at the door and Douglas smiled. "This will be Sir Bentham. He wants to inspect his purchase."

I'd met Bentham before. He'd looked at me in a way that'd made me want to run upstairs and scrub my skin, even when I hadn't understood what that look meant. Douglas opened the door. I couldn't hear their muttered exchange, only Sir Bentham's heavy footfalls and the tap of his cane as he walked toward me.

"Stand," he barked at me.

His cold voice would have made me shiver if I hadn't already been trembling. I tried to lift my head, but I didn't have the strength.

"She's not fed for several days," Douglas said. "Like you requested. She's weak."

Bentham scowled, but nodded. "Makes this part a lot easier. Strap her to the table. No money crosses hands until I check the female's still intact. I need an heir, but I won't breed her unless she's untouched."

I struggled as best as I could as I was carried to a wooden table and strapped down on it, arms and legs wide. Bentham walked over slowly, gripping his cane in his fist, his cold gaze moving over my body. He didn't actually need the cane, but I had seen him beat someone with it.

"Underwear off," he said low and gritty. "If the commander's rutted her, the price halves and I add her to my stable of females when I'm done with her. You'll be the stepfather of a whore, Douglas, and not the mother of my heir, like you were hoping."

Douglas strode over, and I could see the fear in his eyes. He leaned in. "You better not have fucked him, *daughter*. If you've spread your legs for that monster, you'll wish you were never fucking born."

He yanked up my gown, revealing my underwear. I thrashed and cried out, causing myself more pain, but I had to fight. "No, don't touch me—"

A male scream rang out behind the door a moment before it exploded from its hinges.

Constantine stepped forward, filling the doorway, tall and radiating the kind of rage that had the power to burn a building down around us. His lips were peeled back, his fangs extended, clothes splattered with blood. Relief slammed through me, the sight of him making my heart pound. "You touch my mate, either of you, and I'll not only tear your fucking hands off, I'll make you eat them."

Bentham reached for something under his coat, despite the warning. Constantine lunged, so impossibly fast. One moment he was in the doorway, the next he was behind Bentham. He twisted the other male's head in an unnatural way, then wrenched it from his shoulders, tossing it aside.

Constantine's chest was heaving, harsh breaths bursting from between his lips as his gaze locked on to Douglas. A female rushed in, spattered with blood as well. The female I'd seen outside with Constantine the day he left. She rushed to me and started undoing my bindings. "You're going to be okay. They won't hurt you anymore," she said, her lavender eyes blazing.

Constantine kept his gaze on Douglas. "You put your filthy fucking hands on my female."

"She's not yours...you haven't—"

"My mate!" he roared. "You scared her and tormented and tortured her. You made her bleed. You made the reason I live and walk and talk...*bleed*." His snarl ripped through the room.

I stared at him in shock, his words hitting me hard, but still he didn't look my way.

Douglas stumbled back. "John said you didn't want her. He lied, I never would've—"

Constantine prowled closer, inch by inch, stalking his prey. "What? Sent assassin after assassin to take me out? Pay someone in my own household to try to take my mate from me? Did you think I'd let you get away with that?"

"You left her!" Douglas cried. "You don't even want Delphine."

Veera growled as she helped me sit up.

"Until two days ago, you thought she was with me," Constantine said.

Douglas shook with fury.

"Take a look at Veera. Who does she remind you of? She looked enough like Delphine to lead your assassins from Roxburgh. And in those three weeks, I got all the evidence I needed. My brothers, my security, they found it all while I led your people all over the fucking territories, taking them out one by one."

Douglas looked between me and Veera, then back at Constantine, shaking his head. "You're lying, you've got nothing."

He hadn't left me for someone else, he was protecting me.

"We've gathered eyewitnesses, collected sworn statements. You don't have as many friends as you think you do, so many of them were more than happy to share what a sick and twisted male you are, Douglas. I have a list of females that were last seen with you, then never seen again, but the still-healing wounds on my mate would be enough for the court to give me grounds to execute. Your uncle's position sure as fuck won't save you, not anymore." He glanced at Veera, a question in his eyes. She was supporting all my weight and nodded in reply. "But now we have all the sick fucking records you kept, of the females you tortured and killed, the ones you bought and sold to twisted fucks just like you. Including Samara," I snarled.

"No." Douglas shook his head wildly, then his gaze sliced to the door.

My mother stood there, her gaze blank. "I've grown tired of all of this." She motioned to the room at large. "I've given the female everything, all your little mementos," she said, her voice cold, emotionless. Then she looked at me. "You deserved better, Delphine." That was all she said, her voice utterly devoid of emotion before she turned and walked away.

Douglas made a run for it, but Constantine caught him easily, restraining him. "I don't think I'll be waiting for a signed execution order. I don't need one, not with all the evidence I have."

"You're making a mistake," Douglas cried. "No—"

Constantine twisted his head with brutal force, like he had Bentham, snapping his neck, then removed it, ending his life.

Finally, he turned to me, and all the rage slid away, replaced by something else as he strode over and scooped me up in his arms. "Thank the fates you're alive. I thought I'd lost you." He was panting hard, breathing shakily, roughly.

Constantine was *breathing*.

And when my head fell to his chest, too weak to hold it up myself, I heard it.

"Your heart, Constantine," I rasped. "It's beating."

Constantine

I held Delphine carefully in my arms as Veera sped for home. "You're safe now, sweetheart. No one will hurt you ever again."

She stared up at me, eyes wide, trying and failing to hide her pain. "Y-you left me."

I shook my head. "Never. You were here." I touched my chest and felt my now beating heart. Something I never thought would happen in my wildest dreams. "The entire time. It was yours. Only yours. You brought me back to life." When I'd heard her scream, my heart felt as if it exploded through my ribs. Now I could feel it, beating steadily in my chest.

"But Veera..."

"She's one of my warriors, a friend, nothing more."

She drew in a shaky breath as her eyes closed briefly. When they opened again, what I saw had me pulling her tighter to me.

"Y-you won't ever leave me again, will you?"

"No, my precious one. I'll never leave you again." And I meant it. I was done with war, with fighting. I'd protected my race for hundreds of years. It was time to live again, with my Delphine.

"I only ran because I couldn't bear to be in your home without you. I couldn't be there b-believing you weren't coming back, that you didn't want me."

"I should've told you what I was doing. I was worried you'd hate me for what I had to do." Rage still pumped through me, but the scent of Douglas's blood lingering on my clothes, the reminder of his death, helped a little to calm me. Veera had taken care of John, and Bentham had just been a bonus.

We sped up the driveway, and I held Delphine close as I rushed her inside. She was badly wounded. Her back was torn open and there were burns on her skin. She was hungry and weak. The checklist of my mate's pain made me want to bring Douglas back to life and end him again, but far slower this time.

Alice gasped as I rushed by.

"I need to clean her wounds," I said and took the stairs two at a time.

My bedroom door was open, and I carried Delphine in and laid her on the bed on her stomach. Alice rushed in behind me and handed me the supplies I needed.

"Prepare some food. She needs to feed but will need to eat as well." Alice gave my shoulder a squeeze and rushed off to do as I bid. "I need to clean your wounds before I feed you and the healing starts. It might hurt."

She nodded as I took the knife from my boot and cut the gown from her body, revealing every slice and bruise and burn. My blood boiled in my veins at the damage done to her.

I cleaned them as quickly and carefully as I could, every one of her muffled whimpers tearing me apart. The thought of her with Douglas, for not only the last couple of days but most of her life, wasn't something I could stomach.

"Has he done this to you before?" I asked.

There was a pause. "No...he never hurt me, but he would...tell me how he hurt others, would make me listen to their screams at the door. Punishment if I angered him. He'd tell me that he dreamed about...about cutting me." Her breath shuddered from her. "And th-the only reason he hadn't was because if he started, he wouldn't be able to stop. He'd end up killing me and I was worth more to him alive."

Fury pumped through me all over again. I couldn't speak for a long time and made myself focus on tending her wounds—until something caught my eye on the bedside table, a long-stemmed red rose. It'd been dried, its crinkled, velvety petals a deeper shade now, and so fragile. It was the rose I'd left on Delphine's pillow that night, I knew it instantly. She'd kept it, dried it, so she'd always have it.

I'd searched for the perfect bloom for so long, desperate to erase the pain I'd seen in her eyes, pain I'd caused, and I realized that night, my little bride had stolen my heart even before she'd brought it back to life, before I allowed myself to see the truth myself.

When I was done, I crawled over her and began the slow process of licking every cut to hasten her healing. "Okay? Am I hurting you?"

"It feels hot, tingly, but it doesn't hurt."

I moved over her body until I'd tended every slice and burn. She'd relaxed some, but I hadn't, and I wouldn't until she'd fed. Carefully moving her over me, I tilted my head and led her to my vein. She was too weak to strike fast, and the slow way her fangs sunk deep had pleasure-pain shooting through me, making me instantly hard for her.

I ignored it. I ignored everything that wasn't ensuring Delphine got what she needed. She moaned softly as she drew deeply on my vein, the weak movements of her body growing stronger with every swallow of my blood.

A growl rumbled from me when the scent of her arousal filled my senses. I'd been without her for three long weeks. Missing everything about her, longing to hear her voice or catch her scent in the house, to see her sweet smile or have those wide lavender eyes on me.

To feel her lips against mine—to sink inside her heat and claim her over and over again.

She bent her knee, her thigh sliding over mine, pressing her hot, wet pussy against me.

"Please," she said against my skin. "I need you inside me, Constantine."

"Seal your bite, sweetheart."

She did, and I carefully rolled her to her side, so her back was to me. Quickly undoing my trousers, I pulled my hard cock free and pressed in behind her. Being careful of her back, I reached around and offered her my wrist. She immediately bit down, causing us both to groan in pleasure.

"Tell me if I hurt you. Promise me," I said against her ear. She nodded as I slid my leg between hers, positioning my cock at her drenched opening. "Ready?"

She whimpered and pushed her ass back, answering me without words.

I gently kissed her throat as I pushed forward, sliding into her with one smooth thrust. Delphine released my wrist and cried out, her pussy clamping down on me instantly, coming before I even had a chance to move. I gritted my teeth and fought for control as her hips rolled against me. She lapped at the bite, sealing that one, too, then threaded her fingers with mine as I rocked into her.

We strained against each other, desperate for more. Her back was already looking so much better, but I refused to risk causing her still-healing body even a moment of pain.

"Bite me," she cried as she pushed back.

I wasn't strong enough to resist in that moment, and I struck. As soon as my fangs broke skin, she screamed, coming a second time, and this time there was no holding back. I came hard inside my precious female, my body shaking, muscles bunching tight.

She finally collapsed against me and turned her head, looking up at me. "Constantine?"

"Yes, sweetheart."

She licked her lips. "I...I never thought anyone would ever truly want me, that when you came for me, I'd disappoint you. I thought you regretted claiming me, that I'd become a burden. I know I'm not Samara, but—"

"I loved Samara. She was my family, my friend." I cupped the side of her still-bruised face. "But I'm in love with you, Delphine. You walked into my world and tore it down, then rebuilt it with you in it. I can't remember what my life was like before you; I don't want to. It doesn't matter. My life started when I took your hand and led you into that garden. Christ, Delphine, you are everything to me."

"You love me?" she whispered, tears welling in her eyes.

"How could I not?"

Her trembling hand cupped the side of my face, then she gently traced the scar there. "I love you too. So much it scares me."

I pressed a kiss to her lips. "You don't need to be scared anymore, little rabbit. I'm here now, and I promise I'll make sure you never have reason to be scared ever again."

Epilogue

DELPHINE

Two years later

I STOOD IN THE GARDEN, the sun safely behind the clouds, and admired my roses. They were stunning this year. Constantine had sourced several new varieties, heirloom roses that were hard to come by. Their heads so heavy with layers of petals they were weighted down, and their perfume was utterly exquisite.

I clipped a couple more and placed them in my basket. This time of year, I liked to fill the house with them.

Across from me, the doors from the library opened, and Constantine walked out, Marcela cradled protectively in his arms. His gaze lifted from our tiny daughter, finding me, and his violet gaze seemed to darken as he took me in.

He grinned when he reached my side, flashing his fangs. There was no containing my shiver. I wanted him. I always wanted him. I looked down at our sweet baby. "What are you doing awake, Marci?" I kissed the little fist she was waving about and grinned up at Constantine. "Did she even cry? Or were you hovering again?"

"I don't hover." He lifted his daughter higher, pressed his nose to the top of her head, and breathed deeply. "She was missing her daddy, so I picked her up."

I laughed. "Or was it the other way around?"

"Okay, fine. We were missing you, so we jointly decided to come and find you among your roses. Besides, our guests will be arriving soon and I want to show you both off."

He took my hand, and we headed back toward the house. His brothers and their mates were coming for dinner. I'd gone from having no friends, and no real family, to being surrounded by so much love, I could scarcely believe it. I looked up at my mate, and my heart filled like it always did. "Thank you, Constantine, for this life."

He stopped suddenly and gripped the back of my neck, tilting my head to look into my eyes. "It's me, Delphine, who will forever be thankful to you. If we never met, if I'd never claimed you, or the fates chose someone else for you...you, my precious one, would still have found a way to make a wonderful life." He shook his head. "But me? I was nothing. I was death and blood and pain, I was empty, and I'd still be that now if the fates hadn't taken pity on me. My little bride, so fucking fearless in the face of the monster you were claimed by. Only you could have broken through the wall I'd built around my heart and made it beat again. Only you could have made me the male I am now. Only you could have given me this life. Our life."

I had no words. Like he often did, Constantine stole them from me completely when he said things like that. So I reached up, gripped the side of his throat, and pulled him down for a kiss.

The sound of cars pulling up the driveway reached us, and I smiled against his lips. "Our family's here."

He smiled back, took my hand, and we went to meet them.

Blood Moon Heat

BLOOD MOON BRIDES, BOOK 2

PROLOGUE

Two years ago

Mina

I lay still as my bedroom window slowly lifted.

It was him.

He was back.

He'd been at my window before, the first time was the night of my sixteenth birthday. He'd stood outside, watching me through the pink lace curtains. I'd been afraid, unable to move, clutching the covers to me. He'd stayed out there for several hours, soundless, unmoving, then he'd left. The next day the Vampire Court informed my parents that my mate had come to them, that he was powerful, one of The Five, and he'd notified them of his intention to claim me.

It was a full year before I saw him again. Once again, he'd stood at my window, so impossibly still, his deep violet eyes glowing through the shadows. He'd stayed there, watching me for so long, I hadn't been able to keep my eyes open, and somehow I'd drifted off with that cold, hard gaze burning into me.

I probably should have been scared then, and I should be now, as he opened the window wide and stepped into my room. I'd been expecting him, it was the night of my eighteenth birthday, but he'd never come in before.

My heart fluttered wildly in my chest. My father always said I was too curious for my own good, that fear was healthy, that it stopped beings from doing idiotic things that would get them killed. But I hadn't been made that way. I mean, obviously I felt fear, and the first time my mate came to the window, I'd definitely felt it. But he'd done—nothing.

Was he going to talk to me this time? I inwardly cringed. My bedroom looked like someone had projectile vomited lace and silk all over it, but worse, all of it was in eye-watering shades of pink. Princess-chic my mother had called it. I hated it and I hated pink, or at least, I did now, but that didn't matter to her. It was as if she thought a pink, lacy horror show of a bedroom would make me the female she wished I was? I only hoped the male soundlessly moving across the room didn't think this was a reflection of my personality. I was no delicate little princess.

He stopped at the foot of my bed, and I kept my eyes screwed shut, gripping my covers to my chest, but the way my heart raced, he had to know I was awake. Still, I wasn't afraid, not really. This was my mate. He wouldn't hurt me, right?

My skin prickled and a wave of heat washed over me out of nowhere. I flushed hot, sweat immediately coating my skin. I wanted to shove the covers off, but I couldn't; he was just there and it wouldn't be proper for me to lie here in only my nightgown with him right there.

My mouth was suddenly bone dry. There was a glass of water on my bedside table, but I didn't reach for it. I kept up my pretense of asleep, waiting for what came next.

I listened for the sound of him breathing, but he wasn't, and his heart wasn't beating either, which meant he was very old, or he'd been so badly injured at some point that his heart had stopped. Maybe both. I barely contained a shiver at the thought.

He stayed there, utterly silent, unmoving, while I lay there sweaty and thirsty, and as the hours ticked by, my overheated skin grew hotter, and tingly; my shallow breaths turning to pants.

There was an ache between my thighs that had been slowly increasing as well and now it throbbed. I tried so hard not to move, but if I didn't squeeze my thighs together to relieve the terrible ache, I'd cry. I couldn't bear it another moment and gave in, squeezing my thighs together tight. A whimper escaped. It was small, but as soon as it left my mouth, a growl long and deep rolled over me from the foot of the bed.

Finally, gathering my courage, I opened my eyes and turned his way—but he was gone.

One year later

I was dying.

My body was burning up, and the deep, throbbing pain between my thighs had me squirming in my sheets. I lifted my head, refusing to pretend I didn't know he was there this time.

My mate stood there, at the foot of my bed, his face concealed in shadow. He said nothing, didn't move, not an inch, just watched as I writhed and panted and sobbed in pain.

God, I wanted to beckon him to me, I wanted him to touch me, to help me. He'd done this. Somehow, he was doing this to me. Last time, I'd suffered for days after he left. Sweating and crying, the pain in my lower belly and between my thighs so acute I thought I'd die. In my mind, I'd screamed for him. I'd screamed and screamed, but he never came. My parents didn't know what was wrong with me, and I'd been too afraid to tell them the truth.

His head tilted to the side, studying me coldly, like I was some kind of experiment.

Why was he doing this to me?

I shoved the covers off, too hot to stay beneath them a moment longer. My skin was on fire, my hair plastered to the sides of my face. My nightgown was damp with sweat, sticking to my body, and when I squeezed my legs together, they were slick. Embarrassment filled me, darkening my cheeks.

I stared into the shadows, into those glowing violet eyes. "Help me," I begged, knowing instinctively that only he could take this pain away. "It hurts. Please...help me."

Every year he came here, I felt the connection between us grow stronger. How could he ignore it? How could he let me suffer this way? I shoved my hand between my thighs, pressing my palm to my swollen, slick flesh, desperately trying to ease the emptiness, the agony. I squeezed my eyes closed as another wave of humiliation washed through me. "Please," I said again.

Like last time, when I opened my eyes, he was gone.

One year and two days later

I was drifting off when the sound of my window opening reached me.

My birthday had been two days ago. I assumed he'd taken pity on me, that he'd decided not to come. I'd been wrong. Relief and terror filled me at the same time, and I hated the part of me that wanted this, that had anticipated his visit. What was wrong with me that the moment he left my room a year ago, I'd wanted him to come back, that I'd craved the pain this twisted monster caused me when it'd finally subsided days after his last visit.

Just being near him turned me into someone else.

I gritted my teeth. No, I didn't want to feel this way. I scrambled out of bed, and ran for the door. Not this time. I wouldn't let him do this to me again.

One moment he was by the window, the next he was at the door blocking my escape.

He was only inches from me, the closest I'd ever been to him. He was so tall, towering over me, and broad. His muscles strained his jacket. I took in the rest of him. The skin on the side of his throat, the side that wasn't tattooed, was impossibly pale, and the shadows seemed to move with him, concealing his face from me still, all accept those eyes. They glowed bright, boring into me.

The scent of blood hit me, his, I knew it, because my fangs tingled and my stomach growled, and someone else's, not vampire, something *other*. I scanned his body, he wore a suit, but the knuckles of his tattooed hands were grazed and red. For his injuries to still be unhealed, meant he'd done it in the last couple of hours. He'd come right here to me, after he'd done whatever it was he'd done to cause those injuries, to make someone else bleed.

He'd been at the border, fighting the fae, that had to be it; is that why he was late coming to me?

I stumbled back, not from fear of him, but from what he did to me when he came here, from the scent of his blood, and the pain and anguish I suffered for days after he left. The grip in my gut, the connection I felt for him, it was stronger than it'd ever been, and I felt nothing but cold indifference rolling off him in return.

I got the sick feeling I was a curiosity to him, nothing more.

Still, my body ignited, fire burning in my belly, the pulse between my thighs sucking the breath from my lungs. My skin was instantly coated in a cold sweat even as my body went up in flames. My nipples tightened painfully and I crossed my arms over my chest to cover them. Humiliation had me looking at my feet, and as soon as I looked away from him, I was able to think more clearly, and the humiliation quickly turned to anger.

After his last visit, I'd been determined to find out why I reacted this way around him. When my parents had been out, I'd sneaked into the library and taken a book on vampire physiology that I'd been forbidden to touch.

I'd learned the truth.

He was supposed to stay away from me, until my twenty-first birthday, to protect me from this pain, from a "need my body wasn't ready for," the book had said.

Being blood bound under the blood moon stopped it from happening to females. The males however, would feel something like I was now if they didn't mate right after the exchange of blood. The books said, "they would feel increased hunger and a desperate need for release that would turn to intense discomfort and then pain if left unsatisfied." I wasn't sure what mating entailed, and a release of what, I wasn't sure, but if it felt anything like this, it would hurt like hell.

The ache throbbed so hard, I had to grab for the wall. "Are you going to just stand there, watching me until I'm writhing in agony, then leave me suffering for days like you always do," I said through gritted teeth. "Or are you going to help me."

Please, help me. God, I hated that I needed him so badly.

He was quiet so long, just watching, always watching, that I didn't think he'd answer. Screw him. I turned my back on him and strode across the room. I couldn't leave, but I refused to stand that close to him.

"What kind of help do you think you need, Mina?"

His deep, icy voice rolled through the room, stopping me in my tracks. I spun back. "I—I don't know. I just...I need the pain to stop." I was lying, I knew what I needed. Well, kind of, I'd read in the physiology book, though I hadn't fully understood what some of the words meant. But I did know it had to do with mating, that only my mate could stop this pain.

He took a step closer. "You're not ready for me to take the pain away, female."

He was right about that, but anything had to be better than this pain. "Then why are you here, why are you doing this to me?"

Another pause. "Because you...fascinate me."

"And your curiosity is more important than the pain that coming here causes me?"

I couldn't believe what I was hearing. I hadn't expected my mate to be some white knight, like from one of the fairy-tale books I'd read. But I hadn't expected him to be cruel.

"And you don't like it, the pain?"

Was he insane? Dread coiled through me. "Of course not," I whispered, not only scared of the way he made me feel, but truly fearing *him* for the first time since he'd been coming here.

"Explain it to me," he said, his voice growing deeper. "Tell me how it feels."

At his words, I wanted to shrivel in on myself. My body ached and throbbed, craving something, something from him, I didn't truly understand, while he stood there, seemingly enjoying my agony. I straightened and forced myself to look at him, into his cold, dead eyes, glowing from the shadows. I wanted him to see the fear that I knew was in mine, and I wanted him to watch as it drained away, to see it change to anger. I let the pain throbbing through my body, the pain he was causing, fuel it. Then I smiled, the same way my mother did when she delivered a cutting remark. "I don't need to explain it. You'll find out for yourself, I promise you that."

Then I turned away from him again, staring out the window, giving him my back.

Silence filled the room, so acute it was deafening. I thought he'd left, like he always did, but then something cool brushed my shoulder. He was touching me, sliding his fingers over my skin. His chest brushed my back and I gasped, but I refused to run. I stood my ground as he brushed my hair aside and leaned closer.

A rumble vibrated from his chest, moving right through me. "I look forward to it, Mina."

Then he was gone.

Also by Sherilee Gray

Blood Moon Brides:

Blood Moon Bound

The Thornheart Trials:

A Curse in Darkness

A Vow of Ruin

A Trial by Blood

An Oath at Midnight

A Promise of Ashes

Knights of Hell:

Knight's Seduction

Knight's Redemption

Knight's Salvation

Demon's Temptation

Knight's Dominion

Knight's Absolution

Knight's Retribution

Rocktown Ink:

Beg For You

Sin For You

Meant For you

Bad For You

All For You

Just for You

The Smith Brothers:

Mountain Man

Wild Man

Solitary Man

Lawless Kings:

Shattered King

Broken Rebel

Beautiful Killer

Ruthless Protector

Glorious Sinner

Merciless King

Boosted Hearts:

Swerve

Spin

Slide

Spark

Axle Alley Vipers:

Crashed

Revved

Wrecked

Black Hills Pack:

Lone Wolf's Captive

A Wolf's Deception

Stand Alone Novels:

Breaking Him

About the Author

Sherilee Gray is a kiwi girl and lives in beautiful New Zealand with her husband and their two children. When she isn't writing sexy contemporary or paranormal romance, searching for her next alpha hero on Pinterest, or fueling her voracious book addiction, she can be found dreaming of far off places with a mug of tea in one hand and a bar of chocolate in the other.

To find out about new releases, giveaways, events and other cool stuff, sign up for my newsletter!

www.sherileegray.com

www.ingramcontent.com/pod-product-compliance
Lightning Source LLC
Chambersburg PA
CBHW031330060726
47590CB00007B/2420